TRACIE'S REVENGE & OTHER STORIES

ESSENTIAL PROSE SERIES 94

Canada Council   Conseil des Arts
for the Arts   du Canada

ONTARIO ARTS COUNCIL
CONSEIL DES ARTS DE L'ONTARIO

Guernica Editions Inc. acknowledges the support of
the Canada Council for the Arts and the Ontario Arts Council.
The Ontario Arts Council is an agency of the Government of Ontario.

TRACIE'S REVENGE & OTHER STORIES

WADE BELL

GUERNICA

TORONTO – BUFFALO – BERKELEY – LANCASTER (U.K.) 2012

Michael Mirolla, general editor
Guernica Editions Inc.
P.O. Box 117, Station P, Toronto (ON), Canada M5S 2S6
2250 Military Road, Tonawanda, N.Y. 14150-6000 U.S.A.

Distributors:
University of Toronto Press Distribution,
5201 Dufferin Street, Toronto (ON), Canada M3H 5T8
Gazelle Book Services, White Cross Mills,
High Town, Lancaster LA1 4XS U.K.
Small Press Distribution, 1341 Seventh St.,
Berkeley, CA 94710-1409 U.S.A.

First edition.
Printed in Canada.
Legal Deposit – First Quarter

Library of Congress Catalog Card Number: 2012932924

Library and Archives Canada Cataloguing in Publication

Bell, Wade
Tracie's revenge & other stories / Wade Bell.
(Essential prose series ; 94)
Issued also in electronic format.
ISBN 978-1-55071-365-7
I. Title. II. Title: Tracie's revenge and other stories.
III. Series: Essential prose series ; 94.

PS8553.E4567T73 2012   C813'.54   C2012-901197-5

For my grandchildren

Piper, Abbey and Emma Bowie, Jesse Chick,
Sarah and Zander Rampersaud

Contents

Tracie's Revenge

S he was pinch-mouthed, somewhat paranoid and – or, at least, as she'd often been told – completely inconsiderate of anyone's feelings except, at times, those of her son, aged four.

She stood at the kitchen sink in jeans and a yellow T-shirt looking through the small window at a line of white birch trees. Because she could not see beyond them, the birches were in her eyes the start of a forest that went on north probably forever.

The trees and the warm dishwater always combined to make her daydream. She thought of her husband at the saw mill and hoped an accident there would take his life so she could inherit his insurance money and the pickup truck. If that happened she would as instantly as in that moment's reverie transport herself to the city where she'd live in a pleasant apartment overlooking a park and at her own cautious speed select a well-off husband from among those who would court her.

She had no picture of such a man in mind. She did not consider that how a man looked had any relevance to her dream of security and comfort for her and her child.

The telephone rang. She reached for a towel to dry her hands but stopped. It would be no one she wanted to talk to.

She plunged her hands back into the water. As the phone continued ringing, she told herself that getting the dishes done was more important than hearing a gruff voice on the other end of the line demand that she inform her husband that this or that would be repossessed if he didn't make a payment first thing next morning.

Certainly no one would call to be nice. And if someone did, if there were someone who might, she would cut that person off, not wanting to hear niceness any more than threats and intimidation.

When the ringing stopped she became aware of Rambo on the back steps softly banging his head on the metal frame of the screen door. Gene nicknamed the boy Rambo just because of that habit. She knew she should take the child to a doctor to see about the head banging as well as his unnatural refusal to cry that Gene was so proud of. And his inability to utter more than a dozen one or two syllable words. In the city she'd take him to the doctor first thing.

If the phone call was from someone collecting a debt, it would mean Gene wasn't at work. They always went there first to look for him and phoned him at home as a last resort. He wouldn't be in the bar or any other place in town where they could find him. He'd be driving around the country roads with a bottle of rye and his rifle.

The soft banging went on. She poured the dirty water out of the plastic basin, dried her hands and, though she didn't like music or the warped excitement of announcers' voices, turned on the small radio that sat on top of the refrigerator. The noise was to pacify Rambo. The only singer she liked was Hank Williams and they almost never played Hank Williams. Hank Williams was the one strong memory she had of her father, who sang his songs at dances when she was a child, before Social Services came and took her away.

Pretty soon the banging would stop and Rambo would fall asleep on the steps.

She dried the frying pan. Still thinking of her son, she was glad she'd had her tubes tied. She wasn't stupid. She'd always known she was on her way to somewhere and taking one person with her was just right. The man who'd find her in the city would probably have children of his own. He'd leave them with their mother. He wouldn't mind Rambo. No one could mind Rambo. He was so good.

She put the frying pan away.

She knew he wouldn't wake up when she opened the screen door later and slipped out. When he did wake he'd find her sitting beside him. He'd look at her with Gene's big brown eyes and she'd look at him with her big blue ones. It wouldn't matter if they didn't smile. They both knew how phony smiles were, how they hid a person's true intentions, which were always to take advantage of you. There had been few exceptions to that rule in her experience. Watch out for smiles, she warned Rambo as she held him in her arms at the start of every shopping trip in town. She and Rambo didn't have to exchange smiles. They knew how each other felt.

The phone rang again. Maybe it was Gene. If it was she'd tell him when he got home and asked that she was in the yard hanging out clothes and didn't hear the ring. Except she hadn't washed clothes today. She'd tell him she was in the garden, though if he looked he'd see it hadn't been weeded or watered. She'd think of something before he arrived.

Finished in the kitchen she turned off the radio and went outside. Rambo was where she knew he'd be, flat on his stomach on the middle of the three steps. She sat on the top step, leaned against the door frame, pushed long blond hair away from her forehead and closed her eyes.

The sun was hot. She wouldn't be able to stand it for long. She'd soon be as sleepy as Rambo. Then he'd wake up and she'd want to go inside and lie down on the couch. If she did, he'd keep tugging at her until she got up again.

If she lay there dead, she thought, he'd find a way to revive her and pester her to her feet. She'd never seen anyone as persistent as Rambo, not even his father, who always tried to have his way.

The cat walked out of the birch trees and slowly crossed the lawn. He sniffed at Rambo's feet as he climbed the steps. When he reached Tracie she picked him up and threw him onto the grass. She didn't want him licking her. You never knew what he'd been eating out there. Without complaint he disappeared around the corner of the house.

She thought about Gene, about how he said he'd never go back to the city. How he *couldn't* go back to the city. It meant he wouldn't come after her. He was born in the city, lived all his twenty-seven years in the city except for the four he'd been here. He said if he went back he'd be dead inside of a month. There were people he wouldn't be able to stay away from, he'd told her with that look that said if she didn't understand she was stupid.

She understood all right. When she got there she'd have nothing to do with people like that. She knew how to pick out the bad ones. They'd never get her with their gambling and drugs the way they got Gene. She wasn't stupid.

Sometimes when she glanced at the white trunks of the birches and wasn't thinking, she had the impression that she was seeing snow and that something was wrong with her because she wasn't cold. Now, for a moment before the sun forced her to lower her eyes, she looked at their green, shivering tops and imagined war planes just above them. Recently several did appear there, flying together. They scared her to death, roaring out of the forest like that. She still heard the terrible noise in dreams where they didn't drop hundreds of bombs like they would in a war but only one, meant for her.

Gene wouldn't want the child. Rambo was more hers than his anyway. What had Gene done but plant the seed?

She must have been dreaming of the cat because when Rambo woke her, tugging at her T-shirt, she yelled and pushed him off the steps. He landed on his back then rolled onto his stomach. She was angry at the cat first then at the sun because she was sure her face would be red, even if she'd only drifted off for a few minutes. When her face got red it got sore. As she watched Rambo slowly rise to his feet it occurred to her that it was lucky Gene hadn't gotten around to putting in the sidewalk because if Rambo had landed on concrete he might have split his head open.

She stood and rubbed the back of her neck, which was stiff from the way she'd slept.

"Juice," she said then.

"Juice," Rambo replied.

* * *

As she peered into the bathroom mirror for signs of the sun's damage, Tracie considered that, except for the lines around her mouth – lines that had been with her since she was thirteen, she pretty well looked her age. Gene said she was too thin but that was the way she wanted to be. Fat women got nowhere in this life. She'd said that to Gene one time and he'd growled: "Where do you think you want to get?"

She knew what he meant when he said she should be fatter. He wanted her breasts to be bigger, her thighs to be meatier so there'd be more to grab onto.

In the city her man wouldn't think of changing her.

She was at the kitchen table looking at the TV schedule in the newspaper when there was a knock at the back door. The knock frightened her. It was too strong to be Rambo. Her finger stayed on the line that said which guests Oprah would have on.

"Yo," someone said, a man. If she leaned across the table she'd be able to see who it was.

"Hello," he said.

She leaned across the table. He was old, probably in his forties.

"Where's Gene?" the man said. He was tall and thick set, in jeans and a black T-shirt. He had long hair and a moustache. She knew immediately that he wasn't the police or a repo man. He wasn't the type to care about jobs or the law.

Once she was over the surprise of a man appearing out of nowhere, she thought of the thousands of dollars Gene had stashed in jam tins in the basement. Her next thought was for Rambo.

"Gene?" the man asked, smiling in a funny way, as if talking to someone who had a hard time understanding. "I want to see Gene."

"You can't," she said.

"And why can't I?"

"He's not here."

"The disappearing Gene," the man said. "Gene's nowhere."

"He's at work."

"He's not at work."

"He's at work," she repeated.

"I know he's not," the man said. She couldn't see past him to find out where Rambo was.

The man said: "I just want to see him for a minute."

"He's not here."

She wondered why he was waiting on the step when he could open the door and walk in. If she leaned back so he couldn't see her, he'd probably do that, she reasoned, so she remained poised the way she was and hoped he'd stay outside. It would be useless to tell him to leave. She knew very well that he was one of those men you couldn't tell to do anything.

"You sure he's not here?" He was smiling in that funny way again.

"I'm sure." She thought of something. "His truck isn't here. He can't be here if his truck isn't here."

"Right," he said and opened the door.

As he walked in she saw the rifle at his side, pointed straight down. She rushed past him anyway and he made no effort to stop her.

Rambo was in the pile of sand Gene had ordered to make the cement for the sidewalk. The cat was lying on the grass. Both looked at her.

She went back inside. The man was sitting where she'd been sitting. The rifle was on the floor. A set of false teeth lay on the TV schedule, the paper beneath them wet and dark from the saliva they carried.

"Take my advice," he said, gumming his words. "Keep your teeth. Don't let anyone talk you into having them out because false ones hurt like hell. They say you get used to them after a while but it's a well known fact that I'm not a patient man."

Without the teeth his jowls sagged and his moustache seemed to have swallowed his mouth. She looked away from him as she sat down but her eyes went to the teeth and seemed to stick there.

"You won't need false teeth for a while," the man said.

When she looked up she found him studying her. She knew what he was thinking. She knew as soon as they did when men began thinking about that.

"Not for a long time, probably," he went on. "What are you, twenty-four, twenty-five?"

"Twenty-one." Nervous, she stood and walked to the screen door. She thought about the jam tins but forced herself not to picture exactly where they were because you never knew about a man like that, how much of her mind he might be able to read.

Outside nothing had changed.

"Where is he?" the man asked when she sat down again. He sounded like a really old man.

"I don't know," she answered, trying not to look at the teeth or see the tins.

"Think," the man said, sliding his hand slowly across the table.

She watched it come toward her. It was a hand that could snap a neck. "At the hotel, in the bar," she said.

"He wasn't at the bar. Or in the pool hall. Or the coffee shops."

The phone rang. He grabbed his teeth, shoved them in his mouth and sprang to answer it.

"Yo," he said. His voice was deeper now, more bossy.

He listened for a second then said: "Randy."

He listened for a moment more. "I've come to visit you, old bud." And after a pause: "Don't be that way. Where are you?"

He said: "I know you're around. Just tell me where around."

Then he said abruptly: "Fuck you, too," and hung up. Staying on his feet, he asked where Gene would go if he wasn't in the town.

"Driving around," she told him.

"He has a cell phone?"

"No."

"Okay, so he'd have telephoned from town. Now he'd leave and go driving around. That right?"

She nodded.

"Where?"

His voice was powerful. She had to answer. "On the back roads."

"Which ones?"

She told him about a dirt trail that dead-ended in a ravine a quarter mile away. The ravine was wooded and had a trickle of water running through it. "It's Gene's favourite place to go to be private," she said.

"Does he have a gun?"

A devil sprang up inside her. "He'll be shooting rabbits. If he's really mad he might kill a deer. He likes to shoot. He'll shoot at anything."

"What's his truck?"

The devil danced. "A green Dodge half-ton. Ten years old."

He picked up the rifle. "Licence plate?"

She told him the number. He nodded as if not wanting to say anything more because talking might make him forget it.

He left, walking, the rifle at his side. Tracie supposed he'd parked somewhere down the road so Gene, if he'd been home, wouldn't have heard his vehicle in the driveway.

She picked Rambo up from the sand, brushed his clothes and took him into the house. He went to the living room and sat on the floor. From the kitchen table, she could see him rocking back and forth.

Sometimes when she had to think she made a cup of tea and drinking it helped. This time her thoughts came quickly. She didn't need tea.

It wouldn't be stealing. Stealing was stupid because it got you in trouble and she wasn't stupid.

It was her inheritance.

She got plastic grocery bags from under the sink then went down the steep steps to the ill-lit, unfinished cellar and straight to the tins. She opened them one by one, took out the bills and stuffed them in the plastic bags. Back upstairs, she fed Rambo, let the cat in and fed him, then made a peanut butter sandwich and ate it with a glass of milk.

There was an afternoon bus south to Edmonton. She rode it with her father once. They left town in bright daylight and arrived in the dark, hours later.

There was nothing of hers in the house that she wanted to take. In the city she'd buy new clothes for herself and her son. But she remembered that Gene's DVD's were due back today. They were scattered around the television. Rambo silently rocked, his palms pushing hard against the floor, as she gathered them up.

She took the cat outside and watched him run to the trees. Then she put Rambo in the stroller. With the DVD's lying on a faded blanket inside a big straw tote and the bags of money securely tucked in beneath the blanket, they set out to catch the bus.

She kept to the side of the road where there was less gravel and more smooth dirt but still the stroller pushed awkwardly. And the sun was strong. She wished she had sunglasses. When she got to the city she'd buy some to wear in the park. She had never owned sunglasses. She'd hated them because they hid a person's eyes. You couldn't trust anyone who wore them, she'd always believed. She wondered what was coming over her, wanting a pair.

When a wheel came off the stroller she lifted her son out of it and pushed it off the road. In the city she'd buy a better one. She had plenty of money now.

She carried Rambo in her arms then on her back with his arms around her neck. When he became too heavy for her she set him on his feet. She knew walking would be hard for him. She also knew he wouldn't complain. He might stumble and fall when he got worn out but he wouldn't complain.

She thought about his not complaining. As if it might make a difference to him, as if it might somehow help release him from his silence, she said: "You're not Rambo anymore. From now on, you're Paul again."

Where they were now, the ravine was just the other side of the trees that edged the road. She listened for the gunshot. A shot would mean little to anyone who heard it. Everybody shot at something from time to time, rabbits, coyotes, wolves, stray dogs, any animal that was a nuisance.

She couldn't remember when things had worked out so well. It wouldn't matter which man was killed. Either way, Gene wouldn't be in her life anymore. If he did the killing, he'd clear out in a flash, wouldn't think for a moment about her or Paul even when he found the jam tins empty. But she hoped it would be Gene. If it was, there'd be the insurance money and the truck.

She wondered how the insurance company would track her down in the city then decided not to worry about it. Wherever you went, people like that knew where you were.

Coconuts, Hot Sauce,
a Pig Snout in the Stew

Even characters have to eat while they wait for their stories to unfold.

Domingo, for example, sat at his worn wooden table with a meal of chick peas and hard cheese. He thought how nice it would be to have a little ham but there was no ham so instead of dwelling on its absence he thought of how fortunate he was to have oil to sprinkle on the *garbanzos*, more cheese than he could eat and wine from the *bodega*. He imagined how nice a tomato would be, dripping with oil on his plate, but he knew he wouldn't go out to pick one. On cool November evenings the air was unhealthy in the misty, low-lying field. He'd pay for the tomato with tightness in his chest and aching in his bones. And the chick peas would get cold while he was gone. Besides, the tomatoes were not his to pick.

When the meal was finished he would wash the plate and the pot he heated the *garbanzos* in. He would tighten the rope belt that held his trousers up, put on his worn sweater and ageless *americana* and walk the short distance along the narrow street to the village's four-table bar. For the hour that the bar was open he would sip a glass of cognac and talk with his neighbours. On his way home, as he passed the bombed out church that was never repaired after the Civil War, he would reflect on how lucky he was that his rope-soled shoes were in good enough shape to last another winter.

* * *

The temperature is minus twenty-one. Sean doesn't want to go out but he needs food. The car takes forever to warm up. He is furious with the blind or perverse planners who devised a cold climate city in which you needed a car just to get groceries. At the supermarket he leaves the car running. He's afraid that if he turns it off he won't get it started again.

Home with the goods to do a chicken stir-fry, he coats the wok with oil, adds a good amount of curry powder, turns on the burner and goes to another room to catch the headlines on the TV news. He stays to watch the lead story and then the next one, which interests him more. Smelling smoke he rushes back to the kitchen. The curry has burned black in the wok. The stench of burnt curry is repulsive.

The windows are frozen shut. He opens the hall door and swings it back and forth to draw the smoke out. The neighbours will love him for that, he's sure. Days later pockets of curry air linger in the corners of the living room, in the bathroom where the fan doesn't work, in the bedroom, out in the hall.

He fries a pork chop. Now the air is liquid with globules of grease. Frying is fine in climates where doors and windows can be open all the time, he thinks, but not here, not in Canada in the dead of winter. He could skate on the grease on the floor.

He tells himself he'll clean before spring but that turns out not to be necessary. He meets Sandra and moves in with her, sacrificing his damage deposit for the benefit of those who clean for a living. Sandra is a tidy cook who likes to discuss marriage while they eat and plays Farmville on her iPad.

* * *

Aurelia sends her Canadian boyfriend away. He isn't to come back for a week. In the onslaught of his love, Bill has monopolized her. Her friends miss her. Bill chooses to leave Barcelona and spend the week in Cadaques, a fishing village on the Costa Brava.

He enters the dining room of a small hotel fronting the postcard harbour and sits at a table. Elise, a Frenchwoman he silently flirted with in the hotel bar the evening before, picks scum from her *café con leche* and lays it on a piece of bread. With a look of amused disgust he watches her eat it. She glances at him once or twice. He thinks she likes that he has his eye on her.

Finished breakfast, she stands and looks through her purse with her back to Bill while her boyfriend goes to the cashier. Her jean shorts are cut a quarter of the way up from the tops of her thighs. Written small in yellow thread on a lush denim curve is *Semtex*, the brand name of a plastic explosive.

The next day Bill eats oysters for breakfast (but says no when the waiter suggests champagne to wash them down). Over her boyfriend's shoulder, Elise watches him.

* * *

The vacationer from Guadalajara bought half a coconut from the vendor who strode along the beach at Puerto Vallarta calling, "CA-co, CA-co." He cut the meat from the shell, set it in front of her on a paper plate and handed her a bottle of hot sauce. She slopped the green fire onto the coconut then handed the bottle back to him. He approached Sandra. Putting on a smile she waved him away. She hadn't eaten breakfast yet and longed for some coconut but she had no money with her.

As she waited for Sean so they could go and eat, a boy of about nine ran awkwardly toward her, a large iguana draped across his shoulders. With her school Spanish, she understood that he wanted to sell her the iguana. She thought it was dead. Then it blinked.

She was fascinated by the reptile's ridged head and placid, beaded face, but had to explain to the boy that she couldn't take it to Canada. It would freeze to death, she told him. From his quizzical expression, it was clear he knew nothing about Canada so she did her best to act out winter for him: bone-chilling wind, snow falling, ice on the streets, even rime on men's beards. He thought she was comical with her pantomime but wondered what it had to do with making a dinner of his catch. "Now you buy?" he asked in English.

She was sad to disappoint him but he grinned: "No problem. I'll sell it to a restaurant," and ran off happily, though staggering a little under the iguana's weight.

The woman from Mexico City nodded to let Sandra know she'd done the right thing.

Sandra wondered where Sean was. Could he have missed the note telling him where to look for her when he woke up? Her stomach rumbled. Then it churned. She had the runs the night before. Could she make it to the hotel in time now? Then she remembered she hadn't brought the room key. What if Sean wasn't there? What if he was looking for her somewhere else?

The thought of green sauce despoiling cool coconut ... of lizard in a bubbling stew... Walking awkwardly she started toward the closest beach hotel.

* * *

Deep fried sardines eaten with the fingers, one hand on the head, the other on the tail. One of Bill's favourite meals, enjoyed with Aurelia at the Bar La Secueta in Barcelona.

* * *

Sandra and Sean washed their hands at a sink attached to the wall of a neighbourhood dining room in old Puerto Vallarta. There was no menu. They were told what there was to eat but they didn't understand the unfamiliar words. They waited at a table to see what would come.

A plate of appetizers was set between them along with a bottle each of the ubiquitous hot sauce. Sandra asked what the appetizers were and thought she heard *sopes*. They were about the size of a tart. Pulling one apart with her fork, she discovered that they were meat pies. Even without sauce, a cautious first taste brought tears to her eyes. She shook her head. She was sorry but she just couldn't eat it.

They paid for the food they'd ordered and left to find a less combative meal. On the street going back to the tourist hotels and restaurants, they told each other they'd at least had a brief encounter with the real Mexico.

* * *

Aurelia buys *robillons*, a variety of mushroom picked on the lower slopes of the Pyrenees and fought over when they arrive at the markets. As Bill looks on, she excitedly demonstrates how they're prepared. Wash and re-wash, cut into pieces, examine closely for worms, cut out any wormy sections (the worms are slightly whiter than the meat) then sauté in butter. To show how much she loves him, she says, she serves the mushrooms on top of highly prized, extremely hard to get and very expensive steaks carved from a bullring bull.

* * *

Hunks of coarse bread well moistened with wine and sprinkled generously with sugar: a breakfast for Domingo in his house in the Catalan village of Vulpellach.

* * *

Cocido, a traditional Catalan Christmas meal. On an enormous silver serving tray lay out boiled potatoes, boiled cabbage, fat white sausage, fat black sausage, chick peas, chicken giblets, boiled carrots, boiled bacon, boiled pig snout, cock (legs only), pig's ear, boiled calf meat and *pelota* (meatballs). Serve to the sixteen guests at a private party in her famed restaurant, El Gall Blanc, in Vulpellach, very near Domingo's house, by Rosa Maria, Aurelia's friend.

The pig snout sports bristles. It brings luck to the one who finds it on his plate, apparently, but Bill knows as it passes his lips that he's in trouble. Chewing it without gagging is a heroic feat. It is in his mouth for two, three, maybe five or even ten minutes before he overcomes his revulsion and swallows it with half a glass of wine. Someone refills the glass from one of many bottles on the table.

After dessert of a Bisbalenc pastry, unique to the region, with a sweet dessert wine; then black coffee with Cointreau and several varieties of *turón,* which instantly became his favourite sweet of all time; and with warm, quick witted people laughing around him, Bill knows his luck is simply in being there.

* * *

Another lunch with Aurelia at the Bar La Secueta: an octopus trails steam as it's carried from the boiling pot, tentacles tucked neatly beneath it. It turns from pink to white as it cools on the counter. The meat, with a narrow ring of fat around it, tastes surprisingly like ham. They each eat a slice along with a bowl of tasty lentils.

* * *

Melon with *jamon serrano*, leathery, delicious cured ham. Sliced razor blade thin, the ham is eaten with mouthfuls of melon. This is the treat Domingo likes best.

* * *

Sesos and steak tartar very late at night at a packed open air restaurant on the holiday island of Ibiza. Aurelia ordered for them. Bill didn't know what to expect. When his plate arrived his anger smouldered. Brains. She ordered him a meal of brains. Scowling, he said he wouldn't even try it. Aurelia spooned some steak tartar onto his plate, certain he wouldn't eat that either. He tasted it, set down his fork and leaned back in his chair. The meal was Aurelia's well executed revenge for his lack of repentance in their fight that afternoon.

Next morning they lie lazily in their hotel room bed. Bill refuses to make love. She boils with anger. He dresses and leaves. She follows and soon spies him on a bench on the seafront promenade. She is sure he has his eyes on the pretty tourist women.

He gets up and walks away. Again, she follows him. He stops and leans against a lamp post. His crossed arms are like a shield. She berates him for not loving her as he should. Tourists watch. If he had a home other than hers, Bill would catch the next flight back to Barcelona. But he doesn't have a home other than Aurelia's. In Spain without a job and nearly broke he only has her.

* * *

On the broad sidewalk beyond the patio of the Cafe Zurich, at the head of Rambla Canaletas in Barcelona, a vendor has slices of coconut for sale in a white tin tray. From his table on the patio, Bill sees a woman in an ankle-length skirt whom he met at a party. Memory brings the music of a well-played guitar, summer stars and her, in a long skirt then too. She has bountiful Irish red hair. She was shy. Claire is her name, he recalls.

At the party, someone joked that he didn't date women who wore long skirts because he feared they had welts on their legs. The insensitive remark seemed to bring Claire down, as if she took it as a personal reproach. Bill flirted with her a while to see if he could bring her out of her funk. He thought he succeeded and was pleased with himself. Aurelia, though, didn't accept that his motive was what he said it was.

The vendor sprinkles water from a plastic jug onto the coconut slices. Beyond the busy street, tourists sprawl on the grass in Plaza Cataluña despite signs asking them not to. Few travellers from the North understand the difficulty of growing lawns in a hot climate, Bill supposes.

Drinking the last of his bitters, an ice cube bounces against his lip.

In Claire's hand, a coconut slice looks particularly cool and inviting. While she waits at the light to cross to the plaza, he imagines her legs his way: cool, inviting and immaculate.

* * *

Sandra and Sean left Puerto Vallarta to continue their vacation. They wind surfed through a tropical depression. They ate peanut soup at the Georgian Inn, Basseterre, St. Kitts; pumpkin soup at the Bistro Creole in Santo Domingo; cucumber soup at Le Bec Fin, Philipsburg, Sint Maarten. Between meals they looked forward to the next exotic dinner. Sandra felt Sint Maarten would be perfect for a honeymoon.

* * *

Bite, suck, chew; bite, suck, chew: the unadulterated sweetness of sugar cane eaten for energy by Sandra and Sean at the summit of Mount Misery. Roped to their guide, they descended into the crater of the dormant volcano. They were visiting another lovely Caribbean island. It too would be just right for a honeymoon.

* * *

Aurelia puts down her book. "Would you like to hear what Juan Ramon Jimenez says about the pomegranate? 'An exquisite treasure of edible amethysts.' Isn't that nice?"

Bill is eating a pomegranate, delighted by the juice-filled seeds exploding between his teeth.

* * *

"I am strong like Spain for lack of sustenance."

Recalling the quotation from Quevedo, Domingo feels himself strong.

* * *

Empty a can of raspberries into the blender along with a litre of milk ... breakfast of seeds and flavour ... then coffee ... then a long, hot shower. Winston's Saturday begins.

* * *

The irresistible aroma of prawns on the grill in a bar in Cadaques. Bill is there with Elise, the Frenchwoman, on a long weekend in exile from Aurelia. His senses are open wide to pleasure. They watch the sun set on the white-washed parish church. Elise earlier took a picture of him on the shingle beach, the cobalt blue water of the inlet in the background.

* * *

Heaven for Aurelia in the steamy city heat: dining alone with Mozart and a travel book; lemon pork chops, peas with sweet basil, a slice of sharp cheese; a dry sherry before the meal and a liqueur after while daydreaming of refreshing breezes blowing through northern woods.

* * *

At a party with Aurelia's friends at a villa on the Costa Brava, Bill is given the task of opening the oysters. Inexperienced at shucking, his blood reddens his hands. Aurelia saves him by taking over the job. She explains to everyone that there's something wrong with Bill. It's that he grew up a thousand miles from a sea.

* * *

The hors d'oeuvres, nice; the main course, fine; good wine. Dessert, big, rich and gooey. Roxy giggled. She wriggled in her seat then dove into the ice cream like a wide-eyed, almost wild-eyed, child. She wore her velvet dress-up dress, purple as a violet, with a white bib to keep it clean. A dribble of chocolate syrup appeared on her chin. Wiped away, it was replaced by another after her next great spoonful. She quaffed a second glass of sparkling wine, devoured a biscuit dripping with strawberry sauce then once more plunged her spoon into the ice cream. At ninety-two, Roxy knew how to have a good time.

* * *

Katherine added the dried peel of a mandarin orange to the chicken and a little cayenne pepper. The meal was one of Winston's favourites. As the bird roasted, its odours drew him from the room where his desktop sat. Before the screensaver blocked it, an observer could have read a description of Bill ordering the vegetable puree at a black and white tiled restaurant on the Ronda San Pedro in Barcelona, too hungry to wait for Aurelia to arrive.

* * *

To sustain him through his bachelor existence, Domingo had five dinner menus. There were three village women his eyes feasted on particularly well. He had good friends to play cards and dominoes with over a glass of cognac in the tiny bar (the story was that Sancho Panza had dropped in for refreshment there whenever Don Quixote was in the area). He had a cheerful dog, a small black and white television on which he watched news and documentaries (the world fascinated him; he hadn't been more than forty kilometres from home, himself) and in the town the other side of the hill, a whore who was his special friend and with whom he dined every second Tuesday dressed in his timeworn suit.

* * *

Aurelia and Bill buy pastries in a shop in her neighbourhood. The owner of the *pasteleria* is an attractive woman twenty years Bill's senior. Handing him the bag with the pastries, their hands meet and their eyes lock. (But why is Bill interested in yet another woman, Winston wonders?)

* * *

"The Venetians have a proverb," Winston said. "'At table, one never grows old.'"

Katherine raised her glass: "To we who will never die."

"Never die," Winston echoed. He took his first bite of the *merluza*. The almond sauce was just as he remembered it. The fish itself couldn't have been better. Learning to prepare a couple of meals well was one of his few accomplishments from the years he spent on the Mediterranean. Another was a novel, published last year. Mostly, he'd been a beach bum collecting entanglements with the locals rather than treasures from the sand.

Katherine complimented him on the tasty dish.

"As a child," Winston reminisced, "not the worst of our family suppers was the porridge left over from breakfast. Formed into patties, it was fried then sweetened with a dribble of corn syrup."

* * *

A favourite among Domingo's recipes: heat a can of chick-peas; add salt, white pepper, onion and chopped garlic. Fry some bacon. Cut it into pieces and add to the chick-peas. Fry bread in the bacon drippings. Pour the chick-peas and bacon over the bread. Eat with olives, cheese, a tomato from the store and wine.

* * *

For a period in his teenage life, Winston existed on cereal for breakfast and noodles for dinner.

* * *

At an Egyptian restaurant in Cadiz, in the south of Spain, Bill and Elise eat pigeon marinated in lemon juice, stuffed with cracked wheat and spit roasted. It came with eggplant stuffed with rice, minced meat, tomatoes and cumin. It's the final night of their tryst in Andalusia. They hadn't seen each other for a year, not since their weekend in Cadaques. The ambiance is elegant and the music mysterious. The food delicious and Elise beautiful. Nevertheless, Bill is nervous and sad. Doubly sad. Tomorrow he will say goodbye to the effervescent woman who chats about life in Paris, the end of university, a future career and the husband already chosen. Back in Barcelona he will have five nights to wait for Aurelia to return from her holiday on Menorca. Five nights to wonder if she slept with her ex-husband at his summer house on the island, as she threatened to.

* * *

"Do you remember your favourite really awful snack from childhood?" Sean asks after dinner in Sandra's apartment.

"Sure. Velveeta cheese on Stoned Wheat Thins with hot orange juice. We'll have it tomorrow while we watch the hockey game, if you like."

Sean grimaces. They continue to pore over Internet maps as they plan their next vacation, the one that will be their honeymoon. South America interests them this evening.

* * *

At 4:52 a.m. Winston slipped out of bed. He wrapped his heavy robe around him and went downstairs. Without switching on a light, he twisted the dial on the thermostat in the hallway, heard the furnace rumble to life in the basement then continued to the kitchen. He opened the refrigerator, surveyed the contents and took out the butter, the olives, the deli ham slices, a half-round of Edam cheese and a bottle of ale. He elbowed the ceiling light on, set the food on the table, got a glass from a cupboard, a knife and bottle opener from a drawer and the loaf of medium rye from the bread box. With an eddying wind brushing snow against the window behind him, he rested his feet on the hot air register and opened the notebook that was always on the table. After making a ham and cheese sandwich he fed the Bose. Jazz: his preferred response to a restless night.

He celebrated a horn riff with an olive, a drum break with a sip of the good dark ale.

He imagined Aurelia and Bill entwined in the Barcelona night even as their sleep is ravaged by the nightmares troubled love can inspire.

He saw Domingo, content after a Tuesday evening with his special friend.

And poor Sandra ... Or is it Sean who won't recover from the accident in Ecuador?

Which character did he feel closest to, he wondered? Domingo, he supposed.

He poured another glass of ale and drank it as tropical air blew around his legs. He wrote in the notebook that Sandra and Sean's apartment was a bubble of warmth in an ocean of cold.

The alto comped the vibes until they exploded into pieces of glass. Drums tossed the shards around in the air before they came together again to slide home on a sweetly bowed bass. He closed his eyes, thankful to be reminded that perfection existed.

He thought about Roxy. Without a back story and having no narrative future, it would still not enter her head to doubt her existence. Let no ungrateful offspring, no jealous friend, no thoughts of death or fear of inflation stealing more of her pension away trouble her as she parties in the perpetual present.

Winston popped another olive into his mouth, buttered more of the good rye bread and made a second sandwich.

He wrote that the pale dawn was nippy in the village in Spain. He wrote that Domingo forced himself from bed and shuffled to the kitchen to make coffee and eat his breakfast of yesterday's leftover bread moistened with oil.

He wondered if Aurelia will put up with Bill much longer. Is it to spite her ex-husband that she keeps him around? Is it for the novelty of having a foreign boyfriend? Could it be for the uninhibited sex? Might she actually love him?

Sated at last. But one more olive. And another. Then the last one in the jar.

At the living room window he watched snow blow onto drifts already high from a month of storms. Warm and full and one day fat, he mused about himself. Or one day yearning for fried porridge to stave off hunger in the night.

He was in the business of creating futures but his own he couldn't know.

Soft & Easy, Hello or Goodbye

The moment Bowen determined to think no more about Tara was the moment before she called. He was drawing on a bit of cardboard, imagining a face. It felt good to be doing it. He hadn't drawn a creative line since their affair began to wind down.

She asked him to meet her for a drink. He was elated at first then annoyed at having his evening interrupted then elated again, though as she said goodbye her voice offered no hook on which an expectation of happiness could legitimately hang.

His freshly shaved face caressed by the excellent air of the old millennium's final spring, he pedalled south on Calgary's Centre Street then coasted down the hill and the incline of the bridge with the lions. In the black river reflections of the neon logos atop office towers shimmered as if viewed through rippled glass. He slowed, leaned into a right then glided through a left at the Temple of Heaven. He continued into the downtown, knees pumping to *Texas Is the Reason*.

It was a bar he hadn't been in before. Tawny light from phony Tiffany lamps shone on the oiled walnut walls, the fox hunting scenes appeared to be place mats framed and the booths were divided by frosted glass panes with a pattern of transparent ducks in flight.

The lone customer was a white-haired man eating oysters near the back. A bartender and a waiter wearing a bow tie talked together, looking bored. Bowen was glad he'd worn shorts. It wasn't a place where he wanted to look like he belonged.

He drank a beer while he glanced through a newspaper. Then he ordered another.

The white haired oyster-eater left and a couple entered. The waiter and bartender suspended their conversation to drink the woman in. She was six feet, maybe a little more. She wore a blue and white miniskirt, skin tight, striped like a Cinzano umbrella. She was in her mid-twenties, Bowen guessed. Her dark, straight hair was cut short. The bar's trite lighting was perfect for her cover girl's softly glowing, expertly made-up face. The man looked to be in his forties. He wore a blue suit with too much white showing at the sleeves and his black brogues were scuffed. His eyes were at the level of her chin.

Bowen was poised to turn the page when a whiff of perfume stayed his hand and he heard or felt or sensed the woman glide into the booth behind him. Her companion remained on his feet, not pleased that she chose to sit so close to the only other customer, he supposed, but a moment later the guy dropped heavily onto the seat directly at his back.

He turned the page. When the waiter came and the man asked for a Manhattan and a whiskey sour, he imagined the bartender would be happy. It was more a Manhattan and whiskey sour sort of place than a beer joint.

He heard the man say: "I want to help you."

"It's no use," the woman replied. Her piercing, metallic voice startled Bowen.

The man said: "I understand you better than you think. Just open up and talk to me."

"It's no use," the woman said. "There's nobody home."

Bowen's eyes rested on the empty squares of a cross-word puzzle. Annoyed with Tara again, he was thinking of leaving. At the same time, he wasn't blind to his growing eagerness to see her. They'd had their moments. Though not that many, he reflected, annoyed again.

"What do you mean, there's nobody home?" the man asked the woman.

"Don't try to understand. Really, don't try."

"I want to help you, damn it!"

Bowen wouldn't have minded an encore of their best times. She might want that too, he thought. He could have been wrong about what he heard, or didn't hear, in her voice.

"This is just me on a bad day. Go back to work."

It was nearly midnight. Bowen wondered what sort of work the man did.

"I don't want to go back to work. I want to help you."

"How will you help me?"

"With my love."

"Oh, shit," the woman said.

The waiter arrived with the couple's drinks. Capitalizing on the moment, Bowen turned half around for a peek at the woman but the view through a transparent duck was blocked by the man's back. When the waiter paused at his table, he shook his head, thinking he'd wait until Tara showed up to have a third beer. Then he called him back and asked to borrow a pencil.

"It's just me," the woman went on in her odd voice. "I'm squirrelly. Really squirrelly. Really, *really*. Yesterday I was sure it was game over. Today it's like it's the day after game over day and I'm not really here. You know?"

"No," the man said.

"Like I don't have control."

"Of course you have control. You just have to make yourself believe you do."

"You don't understand. You say you understand but you don't."

"Like you're such a mystery." The guy sounded as if wished he *was* back at work.

The waiter brought a sharpened pencil stub. Bowen went through the paper until he found a large advertisement with some white space.

"Relax and drink your drink," the man told the woman.

"I didn't have breakfast and I didn't have lunch and I should eat," Bowen heard as he drew.

"Then order something."

"I would but I can't eat. I don't have the energy. When you called this morning I'd just come from the airport. I had toast and coffee there then the rest of the day I didn't have the oomph to heat soup. I needed caffeine and vitamin drinks just to get ready to come and meet you."

"You were at the airport?" the man said.

"Seeing off friends. I envied them. I wanted to go someplace too. I'm like that at airports when I'm not going anywhere. I remember places where I had good times, like Vancouver or Los Angeles or Toronto or London, and I want to go back. But this morning I realized I couldn't handle being in some distant place alone. I used to *love* that. Wandering by myself, seeing the sites, shopping, playing the woman of mystery at a table for one in a good restaurant. Getting to know someone at a club. Now I'd be nothing but lonely. After a couple of days I'd be totally demented. I didn't have the money anyway, which was just as well. You know, because I really don't have much control. You don't believe me but it's true. I went home. I had a bath. I lay on the couch with afternoon TV telling me I had to have the things my demographic is supposed to die for. And I wanted to cry. But I couldn't cry. I couldn't even cry."

Bowen looked critically at the head he'd drawn, decided it was done and turned to the crossword puzzle.

"Just a minute," the man said. "I'm going to the bathroom."

"I couldn't pay my phone bill because my bank accounts are overdrawn and my cards are maxed."

"I'll be right back. Don't worry."

"I'll talk to myself."

Seven across was "magpie." Eight across, "Dizzy tune, a night in …" was "Tunisia."

"Why do I care if he understands or not?" the woman said.

Surprised, Bowen turned around. Their eyes met through a duck.

"That man's afraid of me," she said.

"Oh," Bowen replied and hastily looked away. He didn't want the man to see them talking.

She started in the moment her friend returned. "I remember thinking that the green of the new leaves was the most beautiful colour I'd ever seen. I wanted to have some things the same shade as the tree outside my window. A blouse or shoes or a toaster or a teapot. I was excited. Since then I've been on a long slide and yesterday was game over day. Today I'm not here. I am really not here."

The man laughed.

"If I had a cat it'd starve," she declared harshly.

"Are you going to drink that?"

"No. Or maybe I should. The alcohol might help me cry. Isn't it funny I can't cry? But, no, I don't want it. Chug it and go to work."

Bowen couldn't get eleven, twelve or thirteen across so he went back to the drawing. As he smoothed the page, he heard a glass bang down on his neighbours' table.

"Double rye and ginger," the man called loudly.

"I'm sorry I don't feel anything," the woman said.

They were quiet until the double rye came. Then the woman burst out: "I can't *feel*! Don't you get it?"

A glass banged on the table again. "Gotta go," the man said.

"I need a thousand dollars. I need at least six hundred dollars for clothes and I need other things."

The man said: "Clothes?"

"To hide my ugliness. Though six hundred dollars won't buy enough of anything to do that."

"Do you want to go now?" he asked. He was still sitting. "I have to go."

"I'm an empty, ugly shell," the woman said. "There's no one inside. I'm sorry. I wish there was."

"I have to get back," the man told her.

"I'm going away!"

"What?"

"I'm going away. I'm going to the airport and I'm going to catch a plane and just go!"

"What do you mean? That's exactly what you said you couldn't do. Where would you go?"

"It doesn't matter. That's the point."

"Of course it matters. Or it would if you had any money."

"I have some tucked away."

"You didn't tell me that. You said you were broke." He sounded like he thought he was being played, it seemed to Bowen.

"It's for emergencies," she said. "Like now."

"Okay, okay. When will you be back? When will I see you again?"

Her voice softened. "I promise I'll be better when I come back. I'll be alive. I won't just stare at television like a zombie."

Like your zombie demographic, Bowen thought with a grin.

"But I need clothes," she went on. "I can't go anywhere without some new clothes. I need at least a thousand dollars more than I've got."

With a sigh, the man hauled himself out of their booth. Bowen watched him cross the room. On his way out the door he stepped aside to let Tara pass.

No smile. No apology for being late. She didn't want a drink. She said she couldn't stay.

Her hair was cropped to the skull. No more the thousand tiny curls that trapped the sun and helped trap his heart. It was a shock, the nun's head. When he reached to touch it, she pulled back sharply.

He waved the waiter off. Behind him the woman asked for a double scotch.

Tara monologued about her conflicts. Did she want to be with her husband? Would she continue with Bowen because, really, she did like him so much? Would she be happiest free of romantic complications for a while?

It was no surprise when she announced that she'd handed the prize to her husband. Still, it stung Bowen to hear it.

"When we see each other socially or at work," she said, looking him in the eye, "you will say or do nothing to remind Teddy or anyone else of our ... peccadillo."

The woman in the other booth laughed.

If Tara's post-affair manners lacked compassion, he forgave her. He knew he wouldn't reclaim his position in that circle of friends anyway. Men and women, they were engineers and geologists with offices in the towers. None were over thirty-five. The fearlessness with which they spent their salaries and bonuses on aggressive cars, adventure holidays, the latest electronic devices and the city's plastic surgeons advertized their gratitude to petroleum.

He was their token artist. When he needed cash he freelanced as an AutoCADD draftsman and during a gig at Shell last year he became friends with Teddy. Not soliciting work in his department again wouldn't be much of a sacrifice.

He thought Tara looked ill though he allowed that it might be the consequence of insipid light falling on a naked scalp. Or maybe he wanted to punish her by diminishing her attractiveness in his mind.

Inside her tidy outfit the label read Jones New York. He knew because they bought it together on a weekend in San Francisco. Underneath would be Vassarette, colour shark.

She had nothing more to say, she declared. He said he didn't either. She retorted that she didn't see how he could have since she was meticulous in calculating the pros and cons and explained her decision to him logically and clearly.

She tapped her fingers on the table then abruptly summoned the waiter.

With the help of a piña colada, she discovered she did have more to say. She talked about her professional rivalry with Teddy. They were so competitive it created tension in their marriage as well as at work. She remembered the day he was promoted over her. She made a terrible scene for everyone in the office to witness. With her emotions in turmoil she was vulnerable and ripe for making a mistake. Unfortunately, the mistake was Bowen.

When she got up, he did too. Putting her hands on his arms, she reached to kiss him. The kiss was soft and easy, the kind that served for hello or goodbye.

He sat down to give her a head start and eliminate the risk of a last glance and twinge of emotion outside on the sidewalk. Rereading a comic strip, he surprised himself by finding it funny this time. He leaned back, feeling released. It was over. He could laugh. And he did.

The woman laughed with him. He'd forgotten her. When she smiled through the duck, she said: "I feel like I lost the lottery. By this much." Her finger and thumb almost met. "Did you lose the lottery too?"

As she relocated to his booth he had a moment to appreciate her long legs up close and in motion.

She asked to see his drawing.

"How did you know I was drawing?"

"I notice things," she said. "I'm not as foolish as I can make myself seem."

"You were pretty convincing with your friend, from what I overheard," he chuckled.

"I can be convincing. I'm an actress sometimes."

"I took you for a model."

"I'm a model sometimes."

Bowen smiled. He found the page with the drawing and turned the paper so she could see it from the proper angle.

"It's me," she said. "It's good. You're a real artist."

"I am," he said. "Starting tonight. Starting with you."

"Sure. I believe that, Mister Artist."

"It's true. I began your face before I knew you existed. I had one line on a piece of cardboard at home. Only one wiggly line but it offered hints and made suggestions for others and in an epiphany I saw the finished portrait in my mind. I drew it after I got here."

"That's some good line," she said mischievously. "Are all your lines that good?"

"You tell me," he grinned. He was finding her very likeable. And her voice was easier on his ears now.

She looked at the drawing again then back at Bowen. "You know what they say, don't you? If you lose the lottery you have to buy a ticket on another one or you won't ever win?"

"I've heard that," he said.

Not missing a beat: "If you need a model ..."

His grin grew as wide as a sunrise.

"You'd want me nude, I suppose?"

"Talk about good lines," he laughed. Sliding from the booth, he offered her his hand.

Prelude to Bach

Montse watched her face emerge from the mist on the mirror as if secrets were being revealed. But of course there was nothing new to see. She pulled a brush through her wet hair and with each stroke said in a small, trailing voice: "I don't care." She imagined a fishing net lost in the sea and sinking with her obligations inside it.

With the murmur of Barcelona in the background, she lay on her unmade bed and repeated the phrase a dozen times more. There were two things in particular she wanted not to have to care about. She recently began working in an unbearably boring office and dreaded having to be there again tomorrow. But more worrisome by far was the niggling fear that what her father would not allow her speak about was true, that she did not possess the depth of talent for the violin that they thought she did.

Rolling onto her stomach, the indigo pillowcase became a bird with outstretched wings floating above a tropical jungle. She gathered her hair in her hand, held it away from head and let it drop and slide along her neck like cool feathers.

She was struck by a whim. She should subject the Bach to another beating then show up at her parents' apartment as she was expected to every Sunday. Instead, she'd go to the zoo.

Tugging the cord, she raised the shutter that covered the balcony door then opened the door to the inviting chaos of cars, motorcycles, scooters and buses and hurried back to the bathroom. The mirror demanded rouge and mascara to erase the tale of last night's club crawl as well as lipstick luminous enough to suit her unusually daring mood.

For her unruly curls, a white butterfly barrette.

In a black satin camisole, wheat coloured platform sandals and a crepe de chine miniskirt, she garnered looks the moment she left her building. She skipped down the steps to the Metro and fished a token from the virtually invisible black satin pouch sewn to the camisole.

A man wearing a brown leather jacket leaned on a pole by the door of the car. He swayed as the train did and tilted as it did on the curves. She kept her eyes on him as she pictured the scene in the living room where she was soon supposed to be.

Her parents and Belita and Rafael discussed the family, trying as always to knead it into some mythological ideal that included her living at home again. Parting the lace curtains, she looked down at the street she walked every day of her life until a month ago.

She could hear her mother cajoling Bel. "*Why don't you quit working? You should have stopped weeks ago. Rafael, she should rest, not work.*" Bel would sigh: "*Don't worry, mama. I don't do too much.*" Papa would intervene: "*Your mother is right.*" "*No papa,*" Bel would say, "*I'm right.*" Papa would snort. Then Mother would ask: "*Why are you so quiet, Montse? Aren't you well?*" To make it appear that she wasn't paying attention, that she couldn't be bothered with family trivia, she'd say exactly what she did last week when her mother asked the same question: "*Santa Clara would be better than a convent school, if it's a girl. After all, it's the nineteen seventies, not the thirties.*"

It upset Papa when the family wasn't complete at the Sunday dinner. He'd be more troubled if he knew she was passing on it not to practice the concerto but to follow a caprice. Mother would worry because she hadn't phoned but if she called it would result in an argument. Then everyone would be upset.

She knew her sister would stick up for her. At her age she was going out with Rafael and missed many Sundays. She well knew the sting of Papa's unjust ire.

She thought the man must be very hot in a leather jacket. At her stop he got off ahead of her. She lost him in the tunnel between stations but when she arrived at the platform for the connecting train he was there. At the stop for the zoo they got off side by side. She lagged behind him as they approached the station where the Paris trains arrived and departed. She assumed he'd be going there. The zoo was a ways beyond the station.

In the sun's delicious spotlight, her step livened with pride in her independence. Her confidence in her musicianship rose too. She would absolutely be ready when the chair at the Palace of Music became vacant next year. They were expecting her and not only because her father was first violin and had been for fourteen years. As a friend of the family, the conductor often listened to her play. He knew how consistent she was. Even after a night in the clubs her concentration didn't falter.

Her rival for the chair was Paloma Benjamín. She hadn't heard her play in a while. Paloma was sixteen and at that age kids advanced by leaps and bounds and in the wink of an eye, so she worried about her.

Self doubt was in Montse's nature. It made her sleep overlong and dribble time away watching television. She scoured progressive magazines and the latest books by anti-establishment women for guidance in defining her role and living her life amid the social and political turmoil of her country's shaky after-the-dictator recovery. That quest was essential but it also punched holes in her practice schedule.

When she paused to peruse the canvas of a white bearded painter perched at his easel, the calm harbour in front of him, the artist gazed at her wide eyed, opened his arms and declared: "*Amor*, your newborn beauty stiffens an old, bent brush so that once again it is able to anoint the female figure with the lustre of love."

Rewarding him with a delicate smile for the delicately erotic *piropo*, she promised herself she'd practice the Bach that night until every note was polished with her love.

Seeing the man in the jacket in line at the zoo entrance surprised and amused her. She extracted a bill from the pouch, unfolded it as the line moved ahead and presented it for her ticket. She didn't mean to follow him but it wasn't completely by chance that she stood across from him at the elands' paddock. When he went to his left, she went to her right and they nearly ran into each other when their paths met. Veering sharply onto another path, Montse took a few steps, turned back to see where he'd gone and found herself face to face with him.

He said hello.

Well aware of the effect she was having on men today, she was cautious. "We were on the same train," she told him. "I thought you were someone I met recently but I wasn't sure." Then she blurted: "You must be very hot in that jacket."

"Are you after my jacket?" he asked pleasantly. "Is this a robbery?"

"No, no, no," she laughed. "I don't know why I said that." His eyes, she noticed, were the burnt umber of her violin.

"I've been sick," he explained. "Even on a day like this I can feel chilled."

"Sick?" She was giving him a choice. He could elaborate or dismiss her as a nosy twit.

"This is the first time in weeks that I've been outside my apartment," he said. "I shouldn't have come out today but I have business ..."

She didn't want to hear a word about business. Not until she got to the office tomorrow and was forced to. "Is you illness serious?" she asked him.

His feet shuffled unsurely before he caught his stride. Montse stayed with him.

"My doctor won't say yes but he won't exactly say no. He's my mother's friend. I suspect he's under her orders not to give me bad news."

He stopped and leaned against a rail. She stopped with him. A few metres in front of them a deer stood mottled by sunlight sieved through eucalyptus leaves.

He asked if she always came to the zoo alone.

"No, never. Today is the exception. A whim sent me, a silly whim initiated by an imaginary bird, if you can believe that." She rubbed the railing then thought of the armies of hands that touched it every day and drew hers back.

Next he wanted to know if he really resembled someone she knew.

"No." Her bare shoulders shrugged. "I have no excuse for making a nuisance of myself. I should let you go on alone."

"Only if you're uncomfortable."

Tropical sparrows chirped in the trees. A flock of yellow thrushes flew to the heart of the foliage and disappeared. A Russian bear lived there, she remembered. Then she realized she was wrong. How could a deer and a bear cohabit?

Coming to the tiger enclosure she skipped ahead and dropped onto a bench as close to the chain link fence as it was possible to get. "That poor animal is forever trying to understand the enigma of its captivity, it seems to me," she observed when the man joined her.

"It gets irritable being cooped up," he said. "I know the feeling."

"Aren't you always surprised by how large it is? I never remember that."

Because the man hadn't been aggressive and didn't seem disturbed in a psychological way, she told him her name when he asked.

"Pleased to meet you, Montse. I'm Tomas."

For the first time, she thought, he took a good, full look at her.

He reached into the inside pocket of his jacket and brought out a notebook and pen. "If I record this moment it won't disappear," he told her. "I do that. I record moments."

She shivered when the tiger reached her. It turned around without breaking stride and continued its peripatetic meditation.

Tomas flipped the notebook closed and got to his feet. As they walked, Montse flexed her fingers. She knew she had great fingers. Faster and stronger than Paloma's.

Just thinking about her rival brought a ripple of anxiety.

While Tomas stood in line to buy fritters at a cart, she found a bench with room for an additional two bodies, squeezed in.

As she ate the sugary *confección,* she glimpsed the Lady with the Parasol atop her high, fountain plinth. She'd loved the statue, robed in nineteenth century hooped skirts, since seeing it for the first time, perched in her father's arms. Growing up, the lady was her model of elegance and sophistication. Recalling the beautiful marble face, hidden by trees from where she sat on the bench, she realized with a start that the statue was of a woman no older than herself.

Tomas said: "Because my memory is sometimes shorter than the lives of those insects that all leap into the air together the instant they're hatched, mate while they're up there then fall to the ground with all the males dead, I'd like to be able to write everything down." His hand swept across the sky to show that he meant the whole world and everything in it.

"Are there really such creatures?"

"Maybe."

Finished her fritter, Montse wondered if she shouldn't ask her father to arrange auditions for her with smaller symphonies in the region, at Tarragona or Gerona or Palma de Majorca. She adored the island of Majorca. She could be quite content living there.

She watched Tomas wipe away the sweat that glistened on his forehead then asked what he did with the moments he recorded.

"I'm always looking for details or anecdotes that might add colour to a play," he explained. "A moment sometimes blossoms into a work of its own."

"So, you write plays."

"I do."

"How interesting. What kind?"

"Kind?"

"Comedies? Tragedies? Absurdist, like they say Arrabal's plays are? Which I don't understand because *Fando y Lis* made *complete* sense to me."

Tomas stood up, looked this way and that then sat back down. "Some of my stuff is political," he said quietly. "I spent a year in London working on a comedy set in Barcelona. To me, it was a light and insubstantial sort of thing but people found more bitterness than humour in it. An English critic saw it in translation and discovered a buried body of between-the-lines anti-fascist commentary. It was an intriguing piece but I had no idea what he was talking about. Anyway, it led to the play receiving a prize. The money underwrote a trip to see friends in the Spanish exile community in Canada. The cold of Montreal in February was a mighty slap that set my head spinning but left me more awake than I'd ever been. I wrote two short plays there, both devoid of philosophy, morality, even basic human warmth. They were staged after I left – in a church basement. Here the censor damned them as nihilistic so they've only been performed in my living room. My last play was about my mother. I thought it was an honest, even flattering portrait of a strongly moral girl battered emotionally by her family's Francoist neighbours but she didn't like it. I tell you, Montse, there's no pleasing a parent."

"That is *so* true," Montse said. "Are you writing another one now?"

"An hour ago I didn't think so."

Was it her imagination, she wondered, or had she seen a hint of slyness, of calculation, in his faint smile?

He stood abruptly and looked around again. This time he stayed on his feet so she got up and looked too. A woman was hurriedly weaving through a crowd on a path coming from the zoo's albino gorilla. Tomas grabbed Montse's hand and she let him pull her along as with surprising vigour he went to meet the woman.

Waves of chestnut hair shimmered around a face Montse could only think of as flawless. When Tomas let go of her hand, she stopped and watched. Holding the woman gingerly, not like a lover, she judged, he kissed the lovely cheeks.

"You told me to meet you by Snowflake, Tomas," the woman said reproachfully. "You're so forgetful. You're lucky I found you."

She reached into her knitted carryall and brought out a package wrapped in brown paper. His hand sunk slightly under its weight. Inclining his head in the direction of a food pavilion he asked if she'd like to have a drink. The woman glanced at Montse before telling him that friends were waiting for her outside the zoo. She kissed him quickly on the lips and walked away.

"My wife, Mariela," Tomas said, watching her go.

Knowing he had a wife skewed Montse's mood. She supposed it was just as well. It was time to say goodbye anyway. She'd have to change her clothes before showing up for dinner. Papa would hate the outfit she had on and she really did not need to be criticized. If she went home to change, though, she suspected she'd pick up a book and stay there.

"Do you trust me?"

The question was so unexpected that she laughed. "A man I've known about as long as those insects of yours live?"

"I'm going to see a young lady. A very young lady. She lives not far from here. We'll take a taxi. We'll be in public the whole time."

His smile was bringing back her adventurousness. She nodded but didn't consider it a commitment. If he did something she didn't like she'd just run.

As it was, they reached the taxi rank at the zoo entrance without her feeling the need to bolt.

"*La Sagrada Familia*," Tomas told their driver then huddled inside his jacket, his arms across the parcel. His breathing was heavy but it normalized after a block or two.

As they raced through the streets, she imagined she was in a scene from his next play, turned into a movie.

He asked in a voice just above a whisper: "Who is Montse?"

She wondered that all the time, she almost said, but supposing he'd think it a juvenile answer to a serious question she provided facts instead. "I finished school this year. I work in an office and hate it. The real Montse is a violinist, soon to be professional. And I'm a progressive."

"A *progré*."

"Absolutely."

The *Sagrada Familia* cathedral with its scaffold-enlaced spires was a century old and far from complete. Montse hated it and said so. "I put so many coins in the donation box as a kid; you know, expecting it to be done next week, and they still haven't figured out what it's supposed to look like."

If that interested Tomas, he didn't show it. Pressing the package to his stomach with one hand, he took her hand with the other and led her through a small park with almond trees and mimosa. He nearly collapsed from lack of breath when they reached the other side and was sweating rivers after dragging her across an intersection. A few steps further on, he pulled her into a bar.

Being Sunday it was closed for business. The lights were off and coming from bright sunlight, all Montse saw in the gloom were some vacant tables near her and a metal counter running toward the back. As Tomas caught his breath, she readied her feet for a sprint back through the open door.

A woman called: "Carmen, your father is here."

So the child, the very little lady, was real and she was his daughter.

"Come, Carmen, he's waiting," the woman called softly.

Accepting that a play must have its twists and turns, Montse let Tomas take her forward. Her eyes had adjusted to the lack of light sufficiently to pick out a woman hunched on a stool, her arms crossed on the counter. Then she saw three men at the last table examining her from sandals to barrette and back again.

"Manuel," Tomas said affectionately when one of the men stood and extended his hand. He shook hands with the other two as well then sat down with them and began to pass the time of day.

Still standing, Montse mused sourly that if Tomas was ignoring her, one of the men decidedly wasn't. Pulling out a chair at an empty table, she sat and crossed her legs.

A light went on in a back room and a girl, three or four years old, wearing a white formal dress, parted the bead curtain with her small hands and went shyly to Tomas. He lifted her up, kissed her and set her on his knee.

Manuel raised his empty glass. The woman who summoned the child went behind the bar, filled a carafe from a cask of *vino tinto* and took it to the men. She went behind the bar again to light a candle. As she brought it to their table, two women, one young, one old, came from the back. She told the young one to fetch glasses for Montse and Tomas and *agua sin gas* for the child. The older one disappeared through the curtain and returned in a moment with a thick, cold potato tortilla on a platter.

Montse ate hungrily. Tomas drank the wine but didn't touch the food.

The man with the searching eyes reached for a guitar that leaned against the wall. Montse jumped at the first forceful chord. The notes were left ringing in her ears as the man took a bite of tortilla and a swallow of wine. Then he surprised her by playing sensitively and peacefully. The strings might have been filaments of silk, she thought admiringly.

The next time the music stopped she found herself listening to Tomas' laboured breathing. He slouched in his chair, his jacket open.

The younger woman made espressos for the men. The older one placed a bottle of cognac on their table. The child sipped water tinted with drops of wine. Finished drinking, she held the glass to her cheek and rested her head on her father's chest. Her brown eyes shining in the candlelight were his eyes, Montse saw. She wondered how she came by her untypical reddish blond hair.

Another man took up the guitar. Understated longing freighted his music. Restrained emotion, Montse had always known, was what gave *cante jondo* its wrenching power. The little hairs at the back of her neck rose as she listened and gooseflesh pebbled her bare arms. Tomas looked like he was being pulled into another dimension by a force he hadn't the strength to withstand.

When the song ended, Manuel waited respectfully for its ghost to leave the room before filling the empty espresso cups with cognac.

The child raised her head and slid to the floor. Parting the beads, she went into the back.

Tomas told Montse he'd set the package on the counter before sitting down and asked her to hand it to him. He pushed it toward Manuel, saying: "It's for Carmen. For her support. And for you for all you've done."

Manuel stripped away the paper to reveal a cardboard box. He lifted the lid and carefully took out four gold sculptures, buffed to a high shine. No one spoke as he set them on the table but Montse almost laughed out loud as she remembered how nonchalantly Tomas' wife, and he himself, had lugged the treasure around. There were gold wafers in the box as well.

"My grandfather hoarded gold, like many of his generation who were in a position to," Tomas told them. "He foresaw that in a country whose future was destined to be as disruptive and bloody as its past, gold alone would ensure financial stability for his family. When he died, my father was already dead, predeceased by his four brothers, all slain in the Civil War. My mother and I inherited his estate."

When they left, the street was noisy, the sidewalk crowded and Tomas spoke so softly Montse had to ask him to repeat his answer to her question. He stopped walking. They were near an entrance to the Metro and people coming and going forced them together until there was almost no space left between them.

"The child's mother – not Mariela, who you saw at the zoo – is from Sweden," he told her. "She was here to learn Spanish and Catalan. We met when she took a small part in one of my plays. After giving birth to Carmen, she disappeared. I suppose she went home. I was living with Mariela. I couldn't confess that I'd fathered a child by another woman but the baby had to be looked after. My father owned several bars which he sold before he died. Manuel was his general manager, the guy who made them all operate smoothly. My father thought very highly of him. To reward him he helped him buy one of the bars, the one we were just in. As a kid, Manuel suffered an illness that robbed him of his birthright to make children. He and his wife were eager to take my child."

"Were you in love with the Swedish woman?" Montse asked impetuously.

She was chilly now that the sun was down and he must have seen her shiver because he took off his jacket and draped it over her shoulders. "I can tell you absolutely that love created the child," he said. "At the same time I loved Mariela."

"Oh."

"When love is generous with you, Montse, it complicates your life."

She hadn't been in love. Not to the point of wanting to have someone's baby. And she had never been so much as infatuated with two people at once.

She was eager to ask more questions. There was a restaurant across the street. If he invited her to dinner, she'd have plenty of time to satisfy her curiosity. For that matter, she thought, why shouldn't she invite him? These days women could take the lead. There was enough money in the camisole pouch to pay for both of them.

She decided that she would invite him. For the moment, though, enveloped in whirlpools of noise and rushing streams of people, she was enjoying being silently bound to him in their sidewalk oasis.

When he bowed his head slightly she thought he wanted to kiss her. But then he began to turn away. She had to speak right then, before he disappeared, but she was so caught off guard that her thinking stalled.

Facing the back of his neck, all she could come up with was: "I hope we run into each other again."

And could have killed herself as he melded with the crowd funnelling down the Metro steps. The words, shallow and meek, offered not the slightest speck of feeling for him to respond to. If he even heard her.

So abruptly alone, it wasn't for several moments that she realized his jacket was still around her shoulders. She waited but he didn't come back. She decided to leave it with Manuel so he could get it from him.

Then it dawned on her. Tomas gave Manuel the gold because he wasn't coming back. Ever. The thought that he wouldn't see his daughter again brought tears to her eyes.

Finally she remembered the notebook. She checked the inside pocket but it was empty. There was nothing in the other pockets either. She was glad. It meant that he still possessed his moments.

She examined the jacket thoroughly for identification of some sort but there was only the label from a shop on Puerta del Angel.

Standing at the curb she watched for the little green light, like an emerald eye, that showed that a taxi was free. Seeing one, she stepped into the street and waved.

Settled in the back seat she looked at the people on the sidewalks going home from their Sunday outings. Soon her eyes narrowed and the figures blurred into a formless mass. When they closed completely, the concerto filled her head.

She heard her violin take flight. Stripping her of sadness and doubt, nervousness and fear, it rose high above the other instruments. It controlled the sky with brilliant pyrotechnics. When the time came, it settled like a bird on a note of pure glory.

She hurried out of the taxi and into her building. She couldn't wait to cradle the violin to her neck, see Tomas' eyes in the colour of the wood and play with Master Bach as he'd never been played with before.

Rational Man at the End
of the Reign of Reason
(Graffiti on the Wall of Literature, #6)

You were attractive, Jupiter Moon, I admit, but wicked, so wicked in the way you were treating me. In my own effing kitchen.

I was anxious to be alone to interface with my genius in the service of mankind, like every Saturday. I assumed you'd leave after breakfast. Instead you launched a monologue that drifted through the hours unrelieved by even one joke or interesting anecdote.

Last night on the neon sidewalk in front of the all-night drugstore where you sold your balsam and paper angels, you complimented me on the brass sleeves on my forearms. Coming closer you admired the mandala tattoo that decorates my nose. Your voice, ripe with flattery then, was sandpaper now.

Running out of ways to diss people on reality TV shows that I don't watch, you started in on the depravity of keeping pets. Salamanders in particular. Kabong, kabong, kabong. On and on. It was too much. I remembered the old magazines I hadn't bothered to toss when I took the apartment. Pulling one from the untidy library beneath the sink,

I held it over the sandbox, shook out a spider and found refuge in the first article I came to.

I read that a rail link to Montenegro was to put an end to Albania's famous isolation. At first the line would carry only freight. Prospective passengers had to wait to see what folks on the other side of the hill looked like as a smugglers' trail rife with bandits, escaped convicts and sour survivalists would be the country's sole umbilicus for humans a while longer.

Well, I thought, that's interesting.

You were still going on about I don't know what. Flinging the magazine into the sink, I got up and dragged you to the door. Before I could push you into the hall you gave me a nasty shove. I staggered back and fell. You scooped me up and kissed me. Your use of tongue was excessive for that time of day, it seemed to me.

I don't do sentimentality, Jupiter Moon. Taking advantage of your post-kiss languor I elbowed you out and slammed the tin door shut. If you'd resisted I couldn't have expelled you. Despite the manly metal on my arm, I'm feeble, basically. Last night your body building buddies took bets on whether I could bench press a marshmallow or not.

I pictured you cross-legged on the grungy hall carpet, happy in your cunning as you schemed to get back in.

Without your voice in my ear, I relaxed. Relaxed, I remembered how, drop by drop, like lazy maple syrup, your charm slimed my intelligence last night. I was weak then. I felt myself weakening now.

Should I dutifully compose the horoscopes people depend on for guidance in their troubled lives or give in to the pleasure-pain of you again?

I slapped my cheek. Of course I would channel the cosmos. With my celebrated gift, I'd translate its advice and predictions as usual and transmit its messages through the earthly ether to the far flung crew that awaits them as impatiently as the world's anal retentives their stock reports and crossword puzzles.

Hate and love, revenge or the fear of it; the desire for good, or evil; the universe's embrace or its dreaded indifference: that was the game of Rogue Roger the Astrologer, aka me.

Scalding coffee black as black and Shostakovich blisteringly loud, these were the pillars of my Saturday pleasure and the backdrop to my revelations. Music was something we touched on in the hours of our courting, Jupiter Moon. You loved only the tunes of the day. Yesterday's hits were trash, you declared, while those from before that you'd deleted from the hard drive in your head. I let you know that as your heart sipped platitudes from the common cup, I gulped the blood of Shosta's profundities.

It was no contest. I'd marinate in a bottomless pot of java and loop the Eighth to eternity, which you wouldn't like at all.

The floor in the hall squeaked. Assuming you were on your way home, I hurried to the bedroom where I stepped on the angel you abandoned in your rush to my bed last night. I lost my balance and fell face first onto the rumpled sheets.

I reached for the laptop on the bedside table, inspired.

Today's message for Virgo: *Get out of those steel toed boots! Go barefoot. Flesh, like the soul, is perceptive. Soles are unfeeling and unmerciful. You must tread sensitively today for an injured angel is in the house.*

Next I focused on Aries. Manic Aries: that was you, Jupiter Moon. You told me so on the street last night as you flogged your angels and horns blared and insults flew from passing pickup trucks.

I'd forgotten Shosta! I was reaching to the other bedside table bent on unleashing the music when I heard you whine. I didn't know it was possible to whine that loudly.

What rights did you imagine you had over me? Our acquaintanceship wasn't twelve hours old.

I padded to the door. Speaking through it, I urged you to consider the neighbours. "I'm tired enough as it is of apologizing every time a salamander escapes from the sandbox, slips under the door then under another door along the hall. I hear the screams, Jupiter Moon. I have to rescue ... I have to pacify ..."

You banged the door with both fists. I yanked it open. You flexed your left adductor longus the way you did in the glare from the drugstore window. I shook my head vigorously to forestall the trance that seductive movement threatened to put me in, as it did then with its irritating consequences.

I said: "Jupiter Moon, I must be totally self-absorbed in order to be totally empty. Only when I'm empty do I grasp the insights from the stars that flash just once then are gone forever."

You flexed again. I shut my eyes. When we left the sidewalk to dance in that swamp of biceps, triceps, pecs, etcetera at your after-hours gym, the flexing all around me made me faint in your arms. Now, even with my eyes closed, I knew you were still flexing and that was enough to trap me. I opened my eyes, saw you and couldn't look away.

I caressed your neck with the metal on my arm. I wiggled the mandala. You laughed. Despite everything, it was sort of good to see you happy.

You took a lipstick from your shirt pocket. It was the waxy yellow of a bell pepper, very striking on your lips. Gamboge, you said the colour was. Digging out more tubes you drew a bold pink circle under your left eye. Under the right, six green lines produced an I Ching hexagram. Your face was again the show I stopped to stare at last night. Like then, I felt compelled to do what you asked.

Then King Henry, I judged from its length, crawled onto my foot and the comforting touch of a salamander's feet creeping across my bare flesh shattered your wicked spell.

I tried to remember. Did I feed the salamanders this morning? Did I water their sandbox? With lightning speed I shut the door and locked it.

Your finger wiggled in the mail slot that hadn't been used for anything since I moved in except to facilitate the delivery of neighbourly hate mail and the landlord's nasty notices. The finger disappeared. Something scraped in the lock and the door flew open so violently it knocked me down.

Jumping up, I searched for signs of a squashing. Fortunately, King Henry had scampered out of the away. I imagined him running for a closet for all he was worth. You held up a hairpin, pointed at the lock, slid your arm around my waist and marched me to the bedroom.

Facing each other on the bed, I said: "Jupiter Moon, I advise on it and know a great deal about it but love is not welcome in my life. It snuck in once. Soon, like a piano squeezed between the walls of an ever-narrowing room, my strings snapped and chaos ensued. Wait!"

Distaff Sagittarian, love is not meant to be painful. Ease up tonight. Don't make your partner cry. Welcome the chaos you arouse in his mind and body. Use it. You will not be sorry. What you want you will get.

"See?" I said. "See how much I know about love?"

I banged my arm bands together. They resounded like dead cymbals.

Your lips formed a gamboge bow. The bow launched an arrow, which was your tongue.

My finger tapped the keys. *Cancer, proceed into the narrow night with ambition and a fearless heart. The dark notes that have bawled and brawled around you will arrange themselves neatly on the staves of happiness to become the wedding march you long to hear.*

"I'm so damned good at this horoscope thing!" I shouted. "More hits every week, Jupiter Moon! Viral soon! Money to follow!"

The finger hopped around the keyboard like a one-legged highland dancer. *Be the best you can be, Aquarius. With your inborn flair, show others what being is all about. The stars guarantee that no one will run away from you tonight.*

Your hand clamped mine. I couldn't pry your fingers loose so I imitated Gandhi and went limp and fell back on the pillow while remaining resistant in my mind. "The eyes of a satyr chained beneath a brothel bed burn with less need than yours do," I breathed.

There was a message there for Leo but with your body pressing my body into the mattress I lost it.

Later, as you lay beside me, your hands passive, I said: "Come with me to Albania, Jupiter Moon. A freight train chock-a-block with gifts for the world will soon set out from lovely Tirana. It's bound to be an event."

One of the smaller salamanders, Prince Jack, I thought, had climbed onto the bed. Gathering up the fragile little beast, I gently set him on your forehead. You shut your eyes but you were brave. I took him off you and laid him on the pillow, where he stayed.

Visions came quicker than the raindrops that cleansed the streets of Fushe-Kruje and Burrel and the sanguineous doorstep of a white and yellow house in Rripe. I saw the vineyards that produce the pinot noir that France would soon import and market in bottles bearing its own sanctified labels.

In the history gallery of the national treasury I saw the three lonely gold ingots, all that remained after the others, a staggering amount of wealth, were carted off in 1913 by a brazen gang of Catalans from La Bisbal and hidden in vaults beneath the waters of the Ter. According to the explanatory tag on the display the precise location of the vaults was still a mystery.

I saw sausages and dumplings. I saw spiced cheese, hams, priceless ancient grains and other valuable harvest commodities such as corn and kidneys that would soon fill shrinking bellies and improve health in realms beyond the sunset.

"We'll have a look at Paris first," I said, by way of a carrot.

Your voice rang out happily: "Oh, city of love, city of light, city of a million pooches messing the sidewalks day and night."

I supposed that was from a song popular with your crowd.

The salamander skittered then settled near your ear as I typed. *Taurus, slip your leash and roam beyond familiar pastures. The adventure you yearn for you is out there. How long has it been since you last surrendered to your bovine urges or unbelted your immense taurine power? You do know what I mean!*

* * *

"Jupiter Moon, it is one of those wonderful September evenings when no tourists remain and the good luck fish are strung from the girders of the Eiffel Tower by those wishing to attract the slippery thing called love.

"In a tailored suit, violet-trimmed gamboge chapeau and nylons with seams artfully askew, you were the sultry, totally untrustworthy heroine of a classic forties' noir picture eyeing a soldier she might like as he waited his turn at the trout vendor's kiosk. Our eyes locked. I said: 'Let me buy you dinner. I know a place where they serve hors d'oeuvres plucked from the best alleys followed by fish ripened on the Tower.'

"Arm in arm, hip to hip, we marched along the Embankment. At the restaurant everyone knew you were a star.

"Like the champagne flutes that toasted our happiness, sparkling minds clinked convivially as we settled in to eat.

"'Liberty is more than just an open door,' a charming couple by the window sang in skilful a cappella.

"'Incarceration,' piped a pretty little girl with a pretty blue ribbon in her pretty blue hair, 'is a lonely cot in an ugly room with not so much as a pot of jam. Neither toast nor tea ...'

"A stooped billionaire cut her off to lament the onerous responsibility of caring for a thousand sweatshops each with a thousand machines.

"You passed the paté, Jupiter Moon. I told you not to worry, that I'd eaten with royalty and not been asked to leave before dessert.

"A woman in a slyly styled peek-a-boo frock addressed the room: 'They take a head shot of you at the door of a club I own. A mask that perfectly reproduces your face is instantly created from the photo. Taiwanese technology. Terribly new. Your partner dons your face and you put on theirs. Nothing matches the strangeness of peering at yourself while you dance in your lover's arms.'

"Above the sizzle of our fish in the pan, the cook complained that his pay made a small space for a drink and a girl to *rhuuuummmm-ba* with.

"When we kissed on Boulevard St. Michel, Jupiter Moon, didn't tiny-lovely lilac panicles mound on your lashes like the snow we were soon to encounter?

"In the shabby closet room in the come and go Harcourt Hotel you flexed as if to mesmerize a cobra. I collapsed on the bed, mesmerized. You lifted me up, dropped me and leapt on me as I bounced.

"Then we were in a rented Ziv on a harrowing mountain road. I glanced at the clock in the dash. More speed was required. At road's end we still had a hike of many kilometres in order to reach the smugglers' trail that would take us the rest of the way in.

"A bridge abutment leaped from the fog. Strangling the wheel, my knuckles white, I avoided its kiss.

"My heavy foot stressed the car to its limit yet we climbed ever more slowly. With clouds enshrouding us, I struggled to make out the low barricade that gave the illusion of separation from the abyss.

"Where there were no barricades, ice concealed the road's crumbling edge.

"The clock stopped. Then only the tattered windshield wipers ticked the hours away.

"'Turn on the radio, Jupiter Moon,' I said. 'They play Shostakovich here. We'll listen to the music and imagine the ecstatic crowds waiting to wave the train goodbye.'

"The radio didn't work."

* * *

I ran my hand between the sheets and found the laptop. *Pisces, do not be afraid to ride the powerful train that is your imagination. Unchained, your intuition leaps to the realm of the sublime. Few understand the seemingly random synaptic conjunctions that produce a multitude of silly ideas then the one that takes all mankind a step forward. You're always thinking, Pisces. Keep it up.*

"Jupiter Moon, every curve introduced us to another of death's deep throats disguised as a valley's unfathomable emptiness. At the summit at last, how I dreaded the descent!"

Libra, you are destined to endure yet another test of your character tonight. Long suffering hero, be brave. Run, don't slink, into the next uncharted valley! You shall overcome! You will survive! You are Libra!

"The road ended so abruptly that the brakes hadn't time to stop us. We skidded toward the drop. You clung to my neck. We screamed in unison ..."

You'd fallen asleep. The hint of contentment on your lips, your hand on my chest, lightly possessive, and the smooth rhythm of your breathing signified to me that you were perfectly at home, that you wouldn't be leaving any time soon.

I admit it. My heart fluttered with cautious happiness.

Warmed by the tropical zephyrs from your nose, Prince Jack slept too. At least I hoped he was sleeping. It was imperative that I get him to the sandbox and wet him down.

But first ... *Trust, Gemini, trust! Although your future is never completely clear, the heavens suggest that success in love will be yours if you but recognize your opportunities and fling yourself at them unabashed. With brazen determination, you will find your one and only sooner or later. Thus say the stars. And though Gemini's often do, the stars never lie.*

I finally unshackled Shosta's fists. They pounded the walls. The neighbour pounded back. You stayed asleep despite the clamour, Jupiter Moon, my new girlfriend slash dilemma. That was good, I thought.

Ignore the complaints, Capricorn. Your heart is just naturally loud. Let the world hear your unmuffled hotrod roar as you race without shame down the drag strip of your days. Lose some, win some, winsome, but don't quit the game.

Capricorn. That was me.

I was marvelling again at how really, I mean really, good I was at the Rogue Roger thing when your eyes opened. I smiled welcomingly. You shrank away. I smiled again, reassuringly. Looking shocked, looking horrified, as if you'd never seen me before, you lunged at my head, locked it in a vice grip and dragged me off the bed. Swinging me around you annihilated my sound system with my flying feet then dropped me, grabbed your angel and fled.

"The Shostakovich, I suppose," I shrugged from the floor in answer to Prince Jack's questioning look.

I picked myself up, limped to the pillow and coaxed him onto my palm. As I watered him down in the sandbox the others came running. They smell moisture from quite a ways off.

Wonderful creatures, salamanders, I thought.

Bandwagon

As soon as my feet touched the floor the stranger ordered me to march. That was how he'd bring me up, he declared: if he thought it was a good thing to do, I would do it. Marching, it appeared, was something I would do. Large, with cropped sandy hair, he smiled but didn't look friendly. As my mother frowned sleepily from the bed, I marched on the spot for what seemed like half an hour but was probably about five minutes.

I was seven and didn't like being woken up and ordered about by strangers. To explain his presence in our bedroom my mother introduced him as the man who just got out of the army, as if I'd know who she meant. I didn't. I hadn't heard that anyone we knew was in the army.

We sat on the edge of the bed, my mother and I flanking him. He gripped her knee, put an arm around my shoulders, and told us a story.

When he signed up for the military, he said, he was a hundred and forty-five pound beanpole. He had never in his life done an exercise because he hated breaking a sweat. Of course his worst nightmare came true. They made him a drill instructor. Since it was the thing to do under the circumstances, he applied himself and six years and a minor war later he showed two twelve on the scales and was so proud of his amazing physique that he wished he could live his life without clothes.

He lay back on the bed and said my mother would fill me in on the rest of the story. She pointed to him as if he was a new piece of furniture she wasn't sure she liked and revealed that he was my father. That was jolting. I'd never thought I had one.

Because it was what fathers did, he said, he'd make sure I exercised conscientiously so I'd be proud of my body when I was older. Sitting up, he showed me his teeth the way a dog does when it imitates a human grin.

My mother liked to sleep late but she had to give up that pleasure and drag herself to the kitchen early to fix the man's breakfast. As he wolfed oatmeal porridge with brown sugar and heavy cream, runny eggs with bacon, two pancakes with butter and maple syrup plus white toast with sugary jam, and gulped a glass of juice, a glass of milk and a mug of coffee, she made the lunch of roast beef sandwiches with mayonnaise and hot relish that he took to work each day.

The sight of food she loathed combined with its bludgeoning smells made her nauseous morning after morning until she learned to pretend that she was a cook-waitress in a truck stop cafe. Not only did that harden her to the job of preparing the same heap of fat, sugar and grease every day, it let her think of him as someone to forget the moment he walked out the door.

Before he came, we ate bread and chocolate in the mornings in the bed I'd always slept in: hers. Sometimes a man was with us. My mother referred to him as my uncle. When I was four, I made no secret of wanting to be a girl so my uncle would feed me the chocolate coated doughnuts he brought us the way he fed them to her, holding them to her mouth so she wouldn't get her fingers dirty. He'd point out that I couldn't be a girl because I had a *piruli*. He'd say that if I ate lots and lots of chocolate I'd be big like him someday and it would be big like his. What did that have to do with wanting to be fed so I wouldn't get my fingers messy and have to get out of bed and go and wash them? I'd ask every time. He'd laugh his booming laugh that never failed to make me laugh too.

We had the television in the bedroom. Again and again it told us how dangerous the world was. There were endless car crashes. People were hurt at their jobs or eaten by sharks or cougars or those drug dealers' dogs that were bred to strip living flesh from human bones. At the playground kids got mugged. At school they got shot. It wasn't completely safe even at home. Parents threw pots, plates and knives at each other. Television showed it. I didn't know why people ever wanted to get out of bed.

The new man, the one my mother said was my father, bought a cot and made me sleep in it in my own room. If he found a crumb of food on the blanket or a toy or comic that I hadn't returned to its proper place, he gave me a fierce dressing-down. I reasoned that if I wasn't a boy, he wouldn't rag on me so much. In TV families girls got away with everything. Fathers were always on their side.

He moved the television into the living room. While he sat on the sofa watching his favourite programs with my mother, I marched or struggled to do a push-up. His shirt was usually unbuttoned. He enjoyed rubbing his chest fuzz like it was a pet he was fond of.

After he left for work in the mornings we hurried to her bed to eat chocolate. Since the television was no longer in her bedroom, she told me stories to pass the time. They were always about my uncle. He was a pirate scuttling the ships of looting empires, a fighter pilot defending freedom in a good war, the president of a multinational corporation hunted by the assassins his shareholders hired after he gave away all the food his factories produced, or the wise leader of a small country who filled his palace with homeless kids and their mothers.

Sometimes she'd ask if I remembered the chocolate doughnuts. I could tell she missed my uncle. I missed him too though he was fading from my memory.

Her bed was my heaven. There she taught me everything I would have learned in school and more. After the lessons she wrote poetry. I had books, toys and a game console to occupy me. When I heard my father's car in the driveway, I'd rush to my room, stow my stuff in the proper places and pull on some clothes.

He bought me a uniform. It was nearly the same as the one he wore in the minor war, he told me as I received it from his hands. The heavy, scratchy fabric saddened me. He also had a toy rifle for me. I marched through the house in my uniform, the rifle on my shoulder. March march march. March march march.

One evening a spoonful of gravy halted on its journey to his mouth. "No religion holds that love of bed is a facet of virtue," he declared ominously. "No civilization ever claimed that bed is where people belong for more than a few hours a night. I don't imagine any television doctor would describe bed as the highway to happiness, except for a few minutes now and then. I'm certain no army in the world punishes infractions of its rules by sentencing the culprit to a good sleep. Do you understand?"

I said I did and watched the gravy disappear.

Next morning I asked my mother what he meant.

"It's his way of expressing society's need to protect itself from the likes of you and me," she explained. "Don't give it another thought."

He got it into his head that I had to go to school. They argued about that as we ate dessert after the Sunday roast of beef.

"He's not mature enough for school," my mother maintained.

"Unfortunately no school we can yet afford will instil in him the discipline he requires," my father replied.

"Schools teach subversive ideas," my mother declared.

"I will not allow a liberal school to force-feed him ideas," he responded peevishly. "Or baby him the way liberals would. He needs a place with rules and plenty of them, strictly applied."

"He's better off learning here with me."

"Learning what?" he scoffed.

My mother could shout nicely. "If you make him go to a military school, I'll leave you!"

My father was good at pounding the table. "If you insist he go to a public school, I'll never marry you!"

"I won't let him go to any school!" she shot back.

"He'll go to school," he said, "but only the right one."

"Which we can't afford. You said so yourself."

"And I meant it!" He banged the table.

I watched the green Jell-O quake in my bowl.

My mother raised her fist. "Therefore he'll go to the school I choose!"

His face red, he blared: "You're wrong! He won't go to any school!"

I loved the way he fell into her traps. But she wasn't ready to let the game end.

"Futhermucker," she hissed.

"Socksucker," he hissed back.

"Soft rocket. Limp macaroni. Tiny Tony."

"March!" he screamed so he could have the last word. Then he ran to the bathroom.

I marched. March, march, march while I visualized the odd images they planted in my mind in their effort not to swear in front of me.

One afternoon my mother stood at the window, spread her arms to indicate the suburb of look-alike bungalows in the middle of which ours squatted and said to me: "I'd give anything to see the palm trees of my childhood and the orchids and pearly beaches and the ultramarine sea warm as a bed instead of the faux-brick back end of a 7-Eleven. But it makes sense to be here."

"Why's that?" I asked.

"Because your father is a citizen."

"What's that?"

"A citizen is a person they can't kick out of the country. I'll be one if I marry your father."

"Am I one?" I didn't want to be if she wasn't.

"You're a citizen as long as your father is your father," she said.

"As long as my father is my father?"

"Someday you'll understand."

"Like when I'm big because I've eaten enough chocolate?" I joked.

She didn't laugh but I think she wanted to.

About then she began taking pills. Soon she couldn't be happy unless she took them.

"I'd give anything for a chocolate coated doughnut," I'd say to cheer her up when she ran out of pills. It worked occasionally.

As a girl, my mother was a revolutionary in the country with the palm trees. "The revolution made sense but it didn't succeed," she sighed one Saturday morning while she lazily emptied the dishwasher. "As a consequence, I was exiled to this cold land where I'm forced to let a snowman share my bed."

"You're wrong," asserted my father, striding into the kitchen after talking to the neighbour about planting twin trees in their back yards. "I'm hotter than a burning bush, woman. Hot, hot, hot, I tell you."

My mother sent me to my room.

That evening he informed me that I only had to march during commercials. To thank him I managed three half decent push-ups.

They raised his pay. To celebrate, he bought me boots.

"They're like the ones soldiers proudly wear," he said, "only smaller. A whole lot smaller. You have a crap load of toughening up to do and a hell of a lot of growing before you're able to fill the real ones. You've seen mine down there in the basement. How big they are. And heavy. In the war, they were feathers on my feet." He gave me his dog's version of a smile. "Maybe I'll take you to a chiropractor and have you stretched. Would you like that?"

I wasn't worried. My mother would never let that happen.

With the right number of pills, the poetry she wrote was flagrantly erotic. She didn't show my father the magazines the poems appeared in because, she confided to me, their inspiration had nothing to do with him.

Without the pills, her poems exploded with the fury that I felt ripple under her skin as I lay beside her.

I resented not being allowed to sit and watch commercials. I shouted at my father that he was a tyrant. I knew it was a terrible word. He used it for the man the army fought in the war. My mother used it for the man who quashed the revolution in the country with the palm trees.

"Call me that again and I'll cut out your tongue," he barked.

He sounded like a pirate. When he raised his fist I imagined he held a scimitar above his sandy head. He lowered it immediately when ordered to by his captain.

"One day, woman ..." he growled.

He sent me to bed when I laughed.

"Does he hate you?" I asked her next morning.

She was scrubbing the frying pan. "What do you know about hate, little one?"

"It's a primitive emotion but it serves a function," I said, repeating what she'd taught me.

"And what function would that be, my good little man?"

I couldn't come up with the answer so I said: "I hate him. That's all I know."

She set the spotless pan in the dishwasher and led me to her bedroom. "These came in the mail," she said, taking a box of chocolates from a dresser drawer. "I ate one yesterday and for a while I no longer hated anyone."

They were delicious, in flavour and effect. I became a fuzzy balloon floating above an enormous carnival with thousands of coloured lights, which is how I always envisioned the revolution.

"Do you miss it?" I asked.

"Miss what, dear one?"

"Your revolution."

She reached under the bed for her scribbler then leaned back on her pillows. As she daydreamed, I watched her ideas surge through her fingers, into her pencil and onto the paper. When the pencil stopped, she told me to say nothing to my father about the chocolates. She dreaded to think what he'd be like if he ate one, she said.

"Virago piss," he growled when he came home one night. A woman had bought the company he worked for and fired him. "But don't fret," he reassured us. "I'll find a better job. Until I do we'll tighten our belts. We'll spend less on everything except food. I bought steaks for dinner. They're three inches thick. I'll have mine blue."

My mother's shoulders sagged.

He stood with her at the stove sniffing and salivating, unable to contain his lust for meat. "The sizzle is my opera and my rock of rock," he rhapsodized. "It's the melody sung by fighting men across the ages. It's the tune that draws the player from the rink, the dentist from his drill. Oh, what that sizzle does to me!" His body wriggled with anticipation.

"You're a precariously balanced man on a dangerous diet," my mother warned him.

I'd never seen him eat so quickly. Finished the steak, he staggered out of the room muttering, "I'll get another job toot sweet so I don't fall into the habit of sleeping late."

Next morning, to get out of the house, my mother went on a day long shopping trip. My father produced a deck of cards and showed me how to play games with dumb names like lo-ball, hi-ball, acey-deucey one-eyed facey, piggy with a pompadour and worm in the soup. Because he always won, his smug smile was permanent.

The next day he looked for work but even without him things were far from perfect. My mother called the doctor for a refill of her pills. He called it in to the pharmacy but instead of sending the prescription with the delivery person the druggist brought it himself. She invited him to stay for coffee and sent me to my room.

"He stayed too long," I complained later, sitting on her bed. "I hate the druggist."

She was beautiful in a new blue negligee. Her arms went around me. As she held me close, she whispered: "Think of love, not hate, my son."

I tried to imagine love but it didn't work. I didn't really know what it was. "I keep seeing the druggist and feeling hate," I reported.

She reached into one of the bags from her shopping spree. "Here, let's put this on you," she said.

She slipped the negligee over my head. The material was infinitely nicer than my scratchy uniform. I relaxed and forgot all about hate and hating.

Reaching under the bed she brought out a parcel. "This came in the mail," she announced. "Why don't you see what it is?"

I studied the colourful stamps before tearing off the wrapping. It was a box of chocolates. I knew it would be.

"They're from your uncle," she said with a just-between-you-and-me wink.

We ate two each. In no time, I was floating above the fairgrounds. I saw my uncle marching with a rifle on his shoulder. The crowd cheered as he went by. I could hear them.

A book of her poems had also arrived in the mail. She held it up so I could see the cover. Her name, long and rhythmical, was in cool blue letters.

She reminded me that I mustn't tell my father about the chocolates. This time she said he'd be angry because they contained something they shouldn't and probably garburate them.

"They're illegal, like me," she clarified. "If I was married to him I'd be legal because I'd be a citizen. But it's not possible for me to marry him. You know the kind of a man he is."

"And me?" I asked. "Am I still legal as long as he's my father?"

"Poor you." She took me in her arms. "My poor, poor little you."

As she rocked me I felt her happiness die. Wanting to bring it back, I asked: "Why don't we go and live in the country of the revolution?"

"Because it's the country of the failed revolution, little one. We could live there if the forces your uncle is secretly gathering around him are successful this time and the reactionaries are overthrown but the odds are against it, I'm afraid."

I imagined the carnival rides stilled, the lights no longer shining. The fuzzy balloon burst and I fell from the sky.

My father's new job made him happy. He was a foreman with a company that used women only as secretaries. "I make them all march," he told us.

The television was on. He pointed at it and shouted: "Disneyland! That's where we'll go for my vacation! Yes, sir, we're on the bandwagon now!"

"Disneyland?" I said.

"Disneyland is a place children can't resist," he shouted exuberantly.

"I can resist it," I said.

He pointed his finger at me like a gun. "Disneyland might make you normal."

I wasn't worried. My mother wouldn't make me go there. I said: "Why don't you pack your bags and go by yourself?"

His finger fired but the execution was a yawn. I caught the bullet between my teeth and spat it back.

"You little glitch!" Purple-faced, he stomped to the bathroom.

I said to my mother: "What if I cut off his head with a guillotine like in your poem where you die because the druggist refuses to come?"

"The doctor won't write me any more prescriptions," she said. "He told me I had to go off the pills for a while."

I dreamed that my uncle and his men were battling reactionary ships. They had to win. They absolutely had to. His mission was to break us out of the tyrant's dungeon. If he didn't make it, we were done for. At dawn they were going to fry us in an enormous pan.

My boots no longer fit so my father bought me new ones. "These are as good as the generals wear," he boasted, tying them to my feet. "Don't imagine you're a general, though. You won't march that well for a long time to come. You can thank me with thirty push-ups before bed."

At dinner he chewed his meat too quickly and bit his tongue. When I laughed, he took my meat.

"I'd give anything to see a palm tree," my mother sighed.

"Then we'll go to Florida," he burst out. "To Disneyworld, which is a place everyone loves. Yes, indeed. It's a good thing to do so we will do it. After, we'll shoot things in the Everglades."

My mother said no, no and no.

She'd probably prefer Cuba, he remarked sarcastically. He knew about Cuba. One day when he was between jobs he watched *Good Morning America* with my mother. "Cuba is awful," the woman on the program told everyone. "Only Haiti could be worse."

"Haiti," my mother said.

"You're out of your mind," said my father.

"I have needs," she said weakly.

"Don't make trouble," he warned her.

My arms gave out after the fourth push-up. As I lay on the floor I heard her say, "I'm in love with another man." She sounded bad. She really needed her pills.

"Don't make trouble," my father repeated.

"Who's this other man you're in love with?" I asked her in the morning.

She was trying to write but she'd thrown the pencil at the dresser mirror twice so I knew it wasn't coming. "The druggist," she answered bitterly. "But he's no longer my friend. In times of crisis we must find new friends."

I snuggled closer to her.

"You're too old for that," she said, shoving me away.

I couldn't be offended. She wasn't herself. I watched her rummage through the dresser drawers, dump out the contents of her purses, search through the pockets of all the clothes in her closets. She turned every shoe and boot upside down and shook it then crawled to all the corners where a pill might hide.

As I marched that night my father said: "Forget palm trees. We'll drive through Idaho. I'll take fishing lessons and I'll catch the roughest, toughest fish they have in their rough, tough rivers. You do know how to clean fish, don't you?"

"Brute," my mother said.

"Boff off," he commanded.

"Impotent feather dick," she snarled.

"Brute," my father said, hurt in his eyes.

The druggist was my mother's friend again. He delivered the pills regularly and stayed for a while.

Winter was long. Then it was spring. My father got a better job and bought a bigger car. I read my mother's collection of erotica in the shade of the tree he'd planted and watched the neighbour's daughter come and go.

In the fall he sent me to a military academy. My mother vowed revenge and told me later she fed him steak every day I was away. It was only a month. I filched everything I saw so they had to drum me out.

I refused to march when I got home. "I certainly won't," I told my father.

"You will," he insisted.

I stood at attention and told him I wouldn't.

He ran to the bathroom hoping I didn't see his floridly flushing face.

My mother's poems were political now. A book of them came from the publisher. Her name on the cover was in smouldering scarlet.

She kept feeding my father the thick blue steaks he loved. Watching women's cage fighting one evening, he got excited and had a heart attack. When the ambulance took him away I put on one of my mother's negligees. It helped. I almost stopped hoping he'd die.

While he recuperated, marching for his health around the house, around the yard and up and down the streets of our suburb, she wrote a novel. It wasn't about anything in particular. She said it summed up life.

My father never knew about the book. Before it was published he had a second heart attack. The doctor said it was brought on by the marching he did and the extra steaks he had eaten to satisfy his increased hunger from all the exercise. A week later his third attack killed him.

This was my mother's eulogy at his lonely funeral: "Like a doused flame, he briefly sizzled and then went cold."

We weren't destitute. He had insurance and my mother's novel earned a little money. Our food bills went way down. She bought fewer clothes and I'd stopped growing so I didn't have to replace mine as often as before. I didn't need a lot of variety in my wardrobe anyway because I didn't go to school. I wore the same things day after day, basically.

I wished I went to school. I'd walk there and back with the neighbour's daughter if I did.

The druggist retired and went to live on a golf course in the South.

My uncle's parcels stopped coming. When my mother was informed that he was dead, she said she'd never be the same again.

One night she turned off the lights and asked me to stand with her at the window. I was shocked by how frail and drawn the moonlight made her seem.

"I've begun another novel," she announced. "It's called *The Empty Womb*. It's about the revolution that wasn't a revolution. It's about your father who wasn't your father. It's about your uncle who wasn't your uncle because he was your father. Yes, he was your father. It's about the druggist who was my friend but wasn't my friend at all. It's about love's eternal cry echoing unheard."

She asked me to march for her. I put on my father's boots and marched.

"March with a gun," she said.

I brought my father's rifle up from the basement and marched with it on my shoulder.

She asked me to move my cot into her bedroom.

I slept there from then on, the rifle always at my side. She wanted me to keep it close in case the reactionaries came after her or the deportation police beat down our door in the night.

Every morning she vomited. In the evenings she cried. At night she wrote her novel.

"Time is important now," she'd say.

I didn't know about that. I spent most of mine in bed sleeping or listening for the shuffle of boots that would mean the enemy was circling our house or to distant sirens coming closer or the rain or a bird or the voice of the girl next door, and it went so slowly there.

What Happened to the Girl?

said, 2:12 pm, March 15, 2025. That's all I said. She asked me the time and I told her. I threw in the date because it's here, see? Right beside the time. Is there a law against that?

(...)

I didn't think so, though you have to admit it's hard to keep up.

(...)

Other than that? Not a word.

(...)

No, I didn't see her go in. I didn't see her come out, either. Look, I'm hungry and I want to go home.

(...)

I was alone.

(...)

I didn't plan to meet anybody. I'm not usually in this neighbourhood.

(...)

Okay, if you want to put it that way, I had no business here.

(...)

I didn't know the girl at all. She was a complete stranger.

(...)

Not a pretty girl. Common looking would be more like it.

(...)

Of course I was aware that she was beside me on the bench before she asked me for the time. What do you think, my eyes and ears and nose don't work?

(...)

Perfume.

(...)

I did find it odd. But I'm of another generation. Girls her age these days ...

(...)

You obviously know nothing about women. The scent of eau de cologne vanishes quickly. Perfume lingers.

(...)

Because I had a life once. With a woman who wore both.

(...)

Her legs were covered.

(...)

Trousers. Loose trousers.

(...)

I didn't look at her.

(...)

I mean, I didn't look at her in the way you're insinuating.

(...)

She was a body beside me on a bench in a park on a warm Saturday in March.

(...)

A sweater. What do you think, she was dressed for the beach?

(...)

Brown.

(...)

I didn't notice.

(...)

Hardly developed at all, then, if that's what you're getting at.

(...)

A glance or two.

(...)

Believe me, that's all. A few quick glances. What do you think, that I wanted to store away a memory of her to take out and use later?

(...)

I mean take out and use for private purposes. You know what I mean.

(...)

I don't have a camera of any kind and if I did I wouldn't take sneaky photos of anyone. I'm not that type of person.

(...)

A purse? I don't think so. But she did have a paper bag, come to think of it.

(...)

No idea. It could have been her lunch. It could have been popcorn or something else to feed the pigeons.

(...)

How would I know that? Whatever else pigeons like. Are you brand new at your job? I mean, these questions of yours. Did I know she was beside me on the bench? Do I know all the things birds like to eat?

(...)

All right, all right. Don't get upset.

(...)

I don't feed pigeons myself. I have better things to do with my money than buy food for birds. Would I get points if I did? Is there something in the regulations about that?

(...)

A pension.

(...)

Nothing else. Just a small pension. You wouldn't believe how small.

(...)

I don't have a criminal record.

(...)

I've never done anything criminal in my life. Why would I lie about that when you'll soon see for yourself?

(...)

I am not in the habit of loitering. I have things to do with my time. Even you might consider some of them worthwhile.

(...)

But I *wasn't* loitering. I was resting. I was enjoying the warm day.

(...)

I don't loiter! I hate that word. It's ugly. I do not do ugly things.

(...)

I didn't say attractive. I said plain.

(...)

A paper bag in her hands, yes. I have no idea what was in it. Let's not start that again.

(...)

She didn't feed the pigeons. She didn't open the bag.

(...)

I'd have heard the paper rustle, wouldn't I?

(...)

Did I hear her clothes rustle? What sort of question is that?

(...)

If I shift in the seat ... like this ... do you hear anything?

(...)

But will you remember the sound a minute from now? You're being stupid. I'm not afraid to tell you that. Most people would be but not me.

(...)

I wouldn't say I lack respect for authority, no. Though in my opinion it doesn't always deserve respect.

(...)

I wouldn't say I lack feeling, either. Maybe I'm more upset than you think by what happened to the girl.

(...)

Well, whatever it was, it must have been dreadful. All these Public Order vehicles.

(...)

A yellow sweater.

(...)

Brownish yellow. Yellowish brown. I don't remember. More brown, I guess, if that's what I said before.

(...)

Slacks. Shapeless. Plain. Loose fitting. Also brown. What else can I tell you?

(...)

A glance or two, like I said. Maybe three, maybe four. You can't expect me to remember exactly.

(...)

Blonde.

(...)

Flaxen.

(...)

I have no sexual habits.

(...)

Pardon me for laughing but how do you expect me to prove it? I will say this: as hard as you look, you won't find a Miss Beauty Home Companion in my closet. And I'm not a member of any club that rents out that kind of biodroid. But I'm aware that lack of evidence to the contrary doesn't prove I'm celibate. Which I am. In body *and* mind.

(...)

No children.

(...)

Children are fine. I have no thoughts about them one way or another. My wife and I just didn't have any, that's all.

(...)

Look, couldn't it be a coincidence that the girl and I shared a bench? Wouldn't that be the most likely assumption?

(...)

On *my* clothes? Not a trace. Well, maybe they would find a little, come to think of it, because this morning I had a nosebleed and I could have wiped my nose, you know, and then cleaned my hand on my pants.

(...)

I'm not thinking anything. I'm just being quiet. Imagining her drenched in blood gives me pause. After all, we shared a bench.

(...)

Then there was no blood?

(...)

I know I don't have the right to be told. I'm not a relative or a friend. But you brought it up. You implied there was blood.

(...)

I said I was *not* a friend! Shit!

(...)

I use foul language sometimes, sure. Who doesn't? It indicates nothing about my character. You're kind of thick, you know that?

(...)

Age gives me the right to say what I think.

(...)

Okay, okay, no one has the right to be uncivil. I agree. I apologize.

(...)

I do not have a violent temper.

(...)

I already told you. She asked me for the time. Otherwise, she didn't say a word.

(...)

I was not acquainted with her. I told you that, too, didn't I?

(...)

If I saw her on the street first, sure, I could have followed her into the park. But I was already on the bench when she showed up.

(...)

I did not lure her. I didn't see her until she sat down, okay? You're very fond of ugly words. Lure, loiter. Maybe that says something about your character.

(...)

Fourteen, thirteen, twelve ... The way they dress ...

(...)

She *was* dressed plainly. I mean others. They seem older than they are.

(...)

Of course. How could I be alive and not notice young girls?

(...)

Fifty-nine. Soon to be sixty and lose points because I'm getting old.

(...)

She left. Pretty soon after that I left too. There was a rain cloud drifting our way.

(...)

A minute or two. Five. Ten.

(...)

There was no communication between us while we sat on the bench or as she left.

(...)

If I followed her out of the park it was unwittingly.

(...)

I thought I'd go to the department store to wait out the shower. I didn't think I could make it to the train before it started.

(...)

I didn't know I was following her.

(...)

I didn't catch up to her.

(...)

Straight to the store to avoid the rain. That's a normal thing to do, isn't it? Normal people try not to get drenched, don't they?

(...)

I hadn't planned to shop but since I was there I figured I'd pick up some things I needed. Socks. Underwear.

(...)

What do you mean?

(...)

Oh, right. I did duck into the alley first. I forgot that. I wasn't trying to deceive you.

(...)

You're right again, I didn't forget. I didn't think it was important, that's all.

(...)

Boxes, garbage bins, a parked vehicle.

(...)

I might have seen something move. I can't say for sure.

(...)

A van.

(...)

No, no people.

(...)

Well, then, maybe it was a person because the van didn't move and neither did the garbage bins. It could have been a cat knocking over an empty box. Who knows?

(...)

A white delivery van, some years old. Dirty.

(...)

Don't ask me why.

(...)

Because I had to empty my bladder, if you must know.

(...)

I was in a hurry. I didn't have time to find a washroom in the store. These days my plumbing doesn't give me a lot of notice before it fails. I'll soon be wearing one of those damned bag things.

(...)

How can you say I followed her into the alley when I didn't see her go into it? How could I know she went in ahead of me if I didn't see her?

(...)

After that? Straight into the store.

(...)

Twenty minutes.

(...)

I didn't like the prices. They want a fortune for stuff that won't last a month. If you want to talk about a crime, let's talk about socks.

(...)

I am not being flippant. It's a crime against humanity. The poor part of humanity.

(...)

I didn't buy a thing. I left by the same door I went in, crossed the street and went back to the park. The cloud was skirting this part of the city. The sun was out again.

(...)

I suppose I went past the alley. Yeah, I must have. I didn't go into it again, though. I had no reason to.

(...)

The same bench as before. I was sitting there when the first Public Order vehicles showed up.

(...)

Why *should* I have run?

(...)

If witnesses saw me go into the alley and then come out of it, it's because I went into the alley then came out. Didn't I just explain that to you?

(...)

I saw no one. A van. Boxes. Maybe some slight movement, maybe not.

(...)

I don't care if you do think I'm lying. I have the right to lie to you.

(...)

The right to lie to protect myself from harm. It's what people do. It's human nature. It's a natural law.

(...)

Uncooperative? I don't think so but if you say I am in your report then I am, right?

(...)

Antisocial, no. Asocial, maybe. I was called that once.

(...)

I looked it up. The definition fit me okay.

(...)

Not one word. How many times do I have to say it? And I repeat, I have no idea who she was. Is, I mean. I don't know what she was up to other than sitting on a bench holding a paper bag with her lunch inside or the crown jewels or birdseed or whatever the ...

(...)

I *am* telling you the truth. I was joking about the right to lie. I've been truthful so far and I'll continue to be, all right? I have no idea what happened to her and that's it. But I can make up a story if you want me to. A nice bed-time murder story?

(...)

Two hundred and fourteen. You can confirm it when your communications are back up. How long does that usually take? That antiquated device is a joke. Even I can see that. I guess the State's so far in debt they can't afford to buy you guys anything better.

(...)

Two hundred and fourteen, I said. An average count.

(...)

Barely average, then, but fourteen points above the Shadow category means I'm still officially an Average, right? I may be bouncing downhill but for now I'm still an Average.

(...)

I lost points for my divorce. That's automatic.

(...)

A few points for disturbances when my wife and I were at the fighting stage. The apartment block warden was keenly alert to our troubles.

(...)

Five or six. We weren't that bad. Our neighbours didn't complain that often.

(...)

I lost points early because I couldn't finish my education in the time allotted. So I began adult life with no degree or certificate. They tell you it doesn't matter but a lawyer or a social engineer or an administrator, someone like that, has to do a lot of harm before they lose points. For those like me, they slough off like dandruff.

(...)

Sure, but who doesn't speculate? Nobody knows why people with the same point count are penalized differently for the same transgression. And that's just one example of what people wonder about. The rules are so complicated and so loaded with exceptions that only lawyers understand them. Though they don't, really, or why would they argue so much at the trials? All that people at my level know for sure is, one year we've got X number of points, the next year X minus so many.

(...)

I know they do, but they rarely add them for people in the Average category.

(...)

Last year? Three hundred and fourteen.

(...)

Driving intoxicated causing harm. A hundred frigging points off for one offense, my only one for the whole year. Plus I lost my driver's permit permanently.

(...)

I hit another vehicle and hurt someone with a lot more points than me. If it was the other way around, if he injured me, he'd have been penalized ten or fifteen points, maximum, and not a hundred. I'm pretty sure I'm right about that.

(...)

Of course I agree with the system. The weight of the law *should* rest more lightly on the person with the most points. He's the better human being, right?

(...)

I'm not bitter.

(...)

I'm not cynical either so don't say I am in your report, okay? I accept that some people are better than others. Acknowledging that in the legal system was a huge leap forward. Just because there's some mystery about how punishments are determined doesn't make the system wrong. And I'm not saying that so you'll think well of me.

(...)

Maybe what you hear in my voice is jealousy. I admit I envy the ones who were given the Order of the Nation and two thousand points the moment the system came into being. You can't even sue someone with the Order of the Nation. And no matter what harm they do, they get points added every year just for being alive.

(...)

Sure that's speculation, but like I said ...

(...)

I lost points in the past for fighting with my boss. Some points were taken off even before that when the workplace warden put in my report card that I didn't get along well enough with my fellow employees. Then I lost more when I quit the job.

(...)

All right, for getting fired.

(...)

Asocial, yes. I know what the word means. I looked it up.

(...)

Why do you ask that question over and over again? Why can't you leave me alone until you learn what the girl's point count is? I'm tired and hungry and you're giving me a headache.

(...)

If I go to court. That's a *big* if! You don't go to court for sitting on a park bench or pissing in an alley, for Christ's sake. Not yet, anyway.

(...)

Look, it's not illegal to swear. You may not like it but it's not illegal. Yet.

(...)

For collecting charity from society while I was unemployed. I got sick and took my pension before I was at my new job long enough to earn those points back.

(...)

Look, it's functioning again. No, it isn't. Oh, yes it is.

(...)

I'll shut up.

(...)

Yeah, I'm worried. Of course I'm worried. It's very likely she'll have a higher point count than I do, so even though I didn't do a thing to her they'll find a reason to chop some points off me. The blood on my pants, maybe. I shouldn't have mentioned that. If you have it tested they'll find it isn't hers but you might not bother testing it, right? You don't like me so you might say in your report that it was her blood just to have an excuse to push me further down.

(...)

I'm not exposing myself. You do make me laugh. I'm just getting ready to take them off when you say you need them as evidence.

(...)

There! You see? Two hundred and fourteen. I'm an Average man, like I said. I didn't lie to you about that or anything else. Ask them to display my record. Go ahead. You won't find a bit of criminality in it. Only the misdemeanors I told you about.

(...)

Yeah, yeah, I'll shut up.

(...)

What? Eighty-nine? Eighty-nine points? Is that what they said? Is that possible?

(...)

Amazing! An Undesirable! An authentic Undesirable!

(...)

I am not delighted!

(...)

I know it is. It's truly sad. What could she have done to be an Undesirable at her tender age, I wonder?

(...)

Don't push me. I'm going. I'm stunned, that's all. I've never met anyone in the Undesirable category before. Some who were low in the Shadow category but no one with fewer than a hundred points, like her. And to think we shared a bench.

(...)

Okay. You'll say in your report that I cooperated, right? I don't need points taken off because of your personal notion of unacceptable behaviour.

(...)

I promise. You won't see me around this part of town for a long time. Really, I promise.

(...)

Okay, I'm leaving. Do you think I want to spend the rest of the day with you?

(...)

No, you're wrong. I'm not lucky. I'm innocent.

(...)

Goodbye, then.

Moron. It was popcorn in the bag. We did feed the pigeons. Pigeons like popcorn. We talked.

The Trick

All Barnett needed was in the old Ford three-quarter ton. There was food in cans and jars, bread, energy bars, energy drinks, bottles of water and a supply of bottled coffee. He had paperback mysteries, a change of work clothes and a pup tent. The natural gas wells Ananke Resources had hired him to evaluate contained no deadly hydrogen sulfide so there was no need to transport lengths of heavy pipe for a flare stack to burn the gas he'd vent during the tests. And no need of an extra man to help with the labour and act as a safety backup. He preferred to work alone.

The wells were in rattlesnake country. In their own compartment of the tool box were the boots he bought for protection against rattler strikes when he worked in the east Texas oilfields years ago. He was fond of the boots. There was little chance he'd encounter a snake but he was pleased to have an excuse to put them on again.

He drove from his sprawling white brick bungalow overlooking Sylvan Lake to the province's main thoroughfare, twenty minutes away, and turned south toward Calgary. Despite a lingering hangover, it felt good to be on a job. Good to leave the house that was, as the months went by, no less empty without Nicole.

The highway took him by grain and oilseed fields and ranches where cattle clustered sociably and horses, paired up or alone, stood along fence lines. Here and there a pumpjack worked like an iron slave. Occasionally a drilling rig or the shorter mast of a service rig rose against the distant backdrop of the Rockies.

He used to enjoy the drive. Now that normal traffic speed had increased to around a hundred and thirty, too far beyond the limit to suit him, it just made him tense. It didn't help that keeping the old Ford on a straight line required both hands and vigilance.

A wheel alignment wasn't all the truck needed. He would have traded it in years ago if he didn't have such a hard time letting old things go.

There were interchanges on the highway but on its oldest sections the odd municipal road still crossed it, regulated only by stop signs. In the distance a flash of silver on one of those crossroads caught Barnett's eye. The vehicle raised a giant squirrel's tail of gravel dust as it sped toward the highway.

The air, weightless and cool above the still lake while he sipped coffee-with-a-kick on the patio at dawn had become heavy and hot, the light viscous.

A tractor trailer unit carrying black strands of drill pipe in a chained triangle hauled past him at one twenty-five at least. The silver car rushed along the road, its tail tall and proud. He wished he'd thought to bring a cushion to fill the swale that the years had excavated in the seat beneath him.

When he looked again he realized the car wasn't slowing. His stomach tightened. Then his teeth clenched and he stopped breathing.

A second earlier and it would have collided with tons of drill pipe. As it was, it made it safely across the southbound lanes. It crossed the narrow median and the first lane coming north. A heartbeat before it was free to raise another squirrel tail on the far side of the highway, a semi popped it high into the air. A door hung from it. A piece of chrome held the sun in what seemed to be a gap in time.

Barnett didn't see it land. Stiffening his arms, he let the Ford charge into the settling dust. The risk was that the vehicles around him wouldn't hold their line or maintain their speed, but they did.

In the rear view all he saw was a dense brown cloud.

His hand slid into the sports bag beside him. Keeping the wheel steady with the help of his knees, he pulled out a bottle of rye.

East of Calgary he stopped for gas then walked across the service station tarmac to a liquor store. He limited himself to another mickey.

Two and a half hours later he ate chewy pork chops, canned peas and watery mashed potatoes in a country cafe on a secondary highway. He was the only customer.

Was he working around there? the waitress asked.

She moved slowly and carefully, like someone accustomed to exhaustion. Her bulging eyes indicated hyperthyroidism, Barnett thought.

"South a bit," he told her.

"Seismic?"

He shook his head.

She brought him coffee. "Will they be drilling around here again, do you know?"

She was flat, front and rear, barely three dimensional, which added emphasis to her eyes. He stirred milk into the coffee and told her he didn't know.

"We could stand to have crews coming in again," she said. Looking out at the empty road, she told him in one long sentence that she grew up on a farm, became a farm wife and was a waitress because they lost the farm on account of bills they couldn't pay.

Barnett checked into the motel next door before coming to eat. The woman who answered the call bell and seemed to need to talk mentioned that she and her husband had owned a farm. When he finally got the key he went to his room to shower. As he dried and dressed he drank what was left in the first bottle. He was still thirsty but not for the water in the glass by his plate.

A slice of saskatoon pie with ice cream topped off his meal. He figured that eating so much proved he was okay. Alcoholics, after all, didn't eat. Recently he'd been eating very little.

As she refilled his cup it struck him that she was a person who'd forgotten how to smile and his heart went out to her as someone not much different from himself. When he left, she was staring through the window as if something out there might have changed.

He sipped rye from the new bottle mixed with cola from the pop machine in the lobby and watched a news broadcast from Calgary. The semi driver and the driver of the silver car were dead.

He finished the bottle in the dark. Without alcohol, he was afraid he'd lie awake tortured by the crash that was his never ending tragedy. As he waited for it to put him to sleep, though, it did nothing to quell the longing for Nicole that regularly made him insane.

After midnight his eyes fluttered open and a fading dream morphed into the belief that she was waiting for him by the pop machine. Thick-headed, he staggered to the lobby in his pants and socks but no one was there. He watched a few minutes of something silly with zombies and slept again. Waking at four, he brewed the motel coffee and drank it as the sky above the parking lot grew light.

The cafe opened at six. The dinner waitress was now the breakfast waitress. She gave him his steak and eggs then went to the window. It occurred to him that she might still retain the farmers' habit of reading the sky.

Pointing the Ford south, he was already looking forward to the chicken sandwiches and pie she'd packed for his lunch.

Rarely used roads led him across treeless land undulating to a horizon he'd never reach. Having made it through the night, he felt valiant now, the way a self-sufficient man might on the Pampas or the Steppes or in the Outback with no other humans around.

At a weatherworn sign announcing an Ananke Resources well, he left the road for a dirt track and came to an agglomeration of pipes, flanges and high pressure valves in the company's peeling colours. Relieved to be there, he got out, yawned and stretched and watched a red-tailed hawk easy-riding a thermal. When he lowered his head, his eyes went to a loose pile of rocks just beyond the wellhead and the rattler basking on it.

It was a juvenile. Still, it was large enough. Three shovels were permanent features of the Ford: a spade for digging, a grain shovel for hefting and a curled blade for pushing snow. He considered each in turn as a tool for scooping the snake off the rocks and concluded that with any of them he'd just create a disturbance which was likely to send it slithering into the pile to hide. He didn't want it that close to him while he worked.

The long-handled spade would be best for killing it. With luck, he'd chop the head off. He didn't like snakes. On the other hand, it was against his nature to kill if options were available. In the end he chose to sweep it away with the broom he used to clean out the truck box.

He exchanged his runners for the boots. Inching forward, he hoped the vibrations from his steps wouldn't drive it into hiding. His eyes on the tail, he braced for a precision sweep.

He was tired after his poor sleep and from dealing with a steering wheel that had a mind of its own and his timing was off. Also, the boots were stiff at the ankles from lack of use and didn't give as they should have when he lost his balance and twisted half around.

Rattles whirring, the snake launched itself into the air. Barnett felt more than saw it fly past his face. It landed in the sparse prairie grass as his torso hit the rocks.

He limped to the truck. The ankle didn't bother him much but he'd wrenched his knee and it burned. He wrapped it in the tensor bandage from his first aid kit and let it rest but the burning only worsened.

He wanted a drink to keep him focused through the pain but the plan had been not to bring liquor into the field. The plan was to prove he could do without it.

Slowly he wound the twelve inch wheel valve open. The shriek of natural gas escaping through an eighth of an inch hole in a round metal plate in an instrument called a critical flow prover would have deafened him had he not worn effective ear protection.

For ten days he'd collect data obtained with his flow prover, a deadweight pressure gauge and a thermometer. At home he'd compute the numbers and draw lines on light green graph paper to show the volume of gas left in each well. He'd transmit the reports electronically. Hard copies, crimped with his professional engineer's seal, he'd courier to Calgary. Then he'd wait. Ananke was eager to have the information but notoriously laggard in paying for work done.

At another well, Barnett sensed that he was being watched as he read his wellhead pressure gauge by flashlight. Back in the truck he activated the light bar atop the cab. Disoriented by the light, a coyote faced him. Its wide open eyes soon closed, breaking the spell of the light, and it turned and loped judiciously into the darkness.

As a child, he slept to the noise of coyotes. In a bedtime story that his sister made up for him, the coyotes missed the buffalo that used to roam the land and the reason they howled was to guide the big animals back from wherever they'd gotten lost.

Pushing the truck door open, something seemed to push it back. Sweat burst from him. He pushed the door again and it opened normally. He didn't believe in the supernatural but he couldn't help thinking of Nicole.

Finished the well, he set up the pup tent and lay down. He didn't expect to sleep with the knee bothering him but he did and he dreamed that Nicole was leaning against the pop machine in the motel lobby. Flushed with happiness, he hurried toward her. Though his legs carried him forward and she didn't move back, the distance between them always stayed the same. He woke up lethargic and depressed.

Carrying his equipment to the truck after doing another well his knee gave out. He lay on the dry dirt drooling from his open mouth until his heart rate returned to normal. He crawled to the truck, raised the bad leg onto the seat, unwound the tensor and rewound it tighter than before.

He stayed in the cab the rest of the day and through the night. At dawn he ate Brazilian beef from a can balled up in slices of bread. Then he drove to the next wellsite. Hobbling to the well, he felt as exposed to unknown danger as a water strider in the bird bath at home.

Another night he imagined that he'd ventured into the wilderness to confront and overcome his weaknesses, like a warrior. Or, he reconsidered, like any ordinary man who needed to fill his emptiness with a scream he wanted no one to hear.

Energy drinks and bebop from an NPR relay in Montana helped him function the next day. "I'm a foul smelling wretch," he called cheerfully to Nicole, "but I'm dry. Not a sip since I've been out here."

He did want something for the knee, though. As he seldom took more than an aspirin or two for pain, he hadn't stocked the first aid kit with anything stronger. His map showed a town an hour west that was large enough to have a clinic but if a doctor ordered him off his feet for more than a day or two Ananke might very well replace him.

Coulees wrinkled the rounded shoulders of the waterless, uninhabited valley where the next well was located. The tranquility of the valley was heaven-like. He wished he could enjoy it. He set up his instruments, took the first readings then slumped with a book in the truck seat's swale. Too tired to make sense of the first page, he put the book back in the sports bag, flung the bag into the truck box and nodded off.

This time when the curtain rose on a dream he was behind the wheel of the silver car, panicking. The accelerator was stuck and the brakes had failed. He could hit the ditch to stop the car but at that speed he'd die if he did. His one hope was that a gap would open in the corridors of traffic on the highway ahead. Nicole spoke to him but gravel striking the undercarriage erased her words. He woke in a sweat, drank some water and stumbled to the flow prover trying to disregard the thirst the water didn't quench.

Alcohol was constantly on his mind as his knee continued to burn. He told himself that a drink would ease the discomfort. It would also lift his mood and maybe put an end to the disturbing dreams. A sip or two would do it. Just a neighbourly wave and a hand up from the genie in the bottle.

He berated himself for rationalizing like an addict. It would be a one finger wave, not friendly at all. The hand up would be a sucker punch.

Now he reasoned that no matter what the doctor advised, he could at least get a prescription for analgesics, have it filled and be back without skewing his schedule too badly.

Deciding to do that, he sped past the entrance to the next well. Then he braked, backed up and turned onto the lease. Electing to do one more test before succumbing to the pain's demands brought a rush of pride in his mettle.

Number six of thirty-six was a weak old thing. Because it didn't make Ananke much money, it was poorly maintained. Barnett nudged open the heavily corroded valve with his four-foot pipe wrench lengthened with a three-foot lead pipe. Then he had to wait for the well to stop slugging water with its slack gas stream before beginning the test. Later, force gingerly applied was required to close the valve. Too much coercion with the big wrench and cheater could snap the handle off while it was still open. Gaining a few centimeters with each delicate tug, the hiss of the gas was eventually silenced.

The truck's air conditioning quit working a couple of years ago. As Barnett drove toward the town with the windows open, the desiccated air sucked the moisture from his body. But when a stretch of washboard caught the truck, sending it tracking violently sideways, there was enough left for a tsunami of sweat.

His healthy knee banged the underside of the dash. His head hit the roof. Veins in his temples bulged and the muscles in his forearms were like braided wire as he choked the wheel, trying to regain control of the shuddering vehicle. Tools bouncing in the box made a hellacious racket. The right rear wheel left the road, tore through a patch of wild flowers and threatened to topple the Ford onto its side.

It emerged from the washboard in a drastic over-steer. He got it back on a straight line before the narrow road narrowed further and funneled him onto a short wooden bridge across the top of a coulee. More washboard lay in ambush the other side of the bridge. He rode it out. Several miles later the road merged with a two lane paved highway.

Coming to the town, he pulled into a service station. The attendant filled the tank and gave him directions to the doctor's office. Almost as a hobby, Barnett memorized the location of a liquor store in places he thought he might return to one day so he also asked for directions to the nearest one.

It was on the way to the doctor's, a red-roofed cinderblock structure with bars on the door and window. Bordering the parking area a cluster of cottonwoods rose from a hollow that he supposed held snowmelt in spring and rainwater if it ever rained enough.

He hadn't seen a tree in days. Their shade was irresistible. He parked in it and closed his eyes to let them rest.

But they wouldn't stay closed and somehow, each time they opened, he found himself staring at the liquor ads in the barred window.

It wasn't long before he went in.

The store was as familiar as a clubhouse. He picked a twenty-six of his usual rye off the metal shelves then glanced at the vodkas. That was Nicole's drink. She'd had a few vodka tonics while they watched sail boats on the lake and she drew up a list of things to buy at a mall in Red Deer. Before getting into her car she read the list aloud to see if he had anything to add. He didn't but the odd thing was, he still remembered every item.

The young clerk shied away from him and was tight lipped when he handed her a bill then thanked her for the change. It was as if she knew all about him, down to the knot in his gut, and liked none of it.

In the truck he broke the seal, unscrewed the cap, tipped the bottle to his lips and with an enormous sigh enjoyed the burn that surged toward his heart.

He sat in the shade thinking about nothing until an impulse totally devoid of reason sent him back into the store. He paid no attention to the clerk this time, simply dropped a bill on the counter and silently pocketed the change.

The vodka wasn't for drinking. If he didn't know why he bought it, he did know that.

He gathered up his garbage, including the forgotten bag of chicken sandwiches and pie that scudded from under the seat as the truck hopped on the washboard. He took it all to a barrel at the corner of the building.

Sweeping fly husks from the dash, he recalled the June bugs in Texas thick as blizzard snow in service station lights.

He shoved the bottles along the seat so they were out of reach then turned the Ford around. The knee's burn had cooled considerably. He was sure it had. If it became intolerable again at least he knew where to find the doctor. As he sped along the pavement he supposed he should have had a hot meal in a café but he hadn't been thinking about food.

On the gravel, the first bumps bounced the rye to him. The vodka came too, unwilling to be left behind, he imagined. He set the whiskey bottle between his thighs and worked off the cap. Keeping the truck steady with one firm hand, he took a healthy hit to intercept the bubble of melancholy that threatened to escape as a sob.

Ahead, a hawk glided, head down, ready to drop like a stone and kill.

He capped the rye. Grabbing the vodka, he held it to his eye in a symbolic salute to Nicole and how she saw the world. Then he jammed it into his crotch and straightened his back.

He drove with a purpose that was vague at first but became clearer as his emotions froze.

From his research into mourning, he'd learned that mind could play a truly evil trick. Akrasia, the trick was called and the mind played it on itself. It made a person unable *not* to do something even though it was against their better judgment. Socrates saw how it worked and gave it its name. The kid with no criminal propensities before or after shoplifting a chocolate bar could be its victim. It was the devil in *the devil made me do it.*

Barnett saw now that akrasia duped him into stopping at the liquor store. The cottonwoods' shade was its convenient come-on and its trap. It opened his eyes on the booze ads. Plundering his will, it took him through the door.

He might as well have been a zombie.

In his mind's eye he saw the washboard ahead and the narrow bridge across the coulee and was confronted, or, rather, he confronted himself, with a question so crucial the answer would mean everything.

Which would fail first, his nerve or his will to remain in the world?

It had just then popped into his consciousness but it felt like he'd been expecting it since the day Nicole died.

His foot stubbornly pressed the accelerator all the way down.

The motor hesitated and threatened to stall but it caught and the old Ford cut loose as if craving the challenge.

Papers and Pearls

In the mellow gaslight of a red-walled private dining room at Lippard's, in New Orleans, the captain's rolling papers were the orange of the sorbet.

"Might I look at the packet, father?" the excited girl asked the man who had returned from an epic sea voyage just that morning.

"You will not allow any water, not one drop, to touch the rice papers, my dear, as they will be ruined if you do and Papa won't be able to have a smoke with his coffee."

"Papa, yes," she said eagerly, experiencing another eruption of pride. The first had come when their entry into the restaurant garnered gasps from ladies and ahs of envy from men. The second occurred moments later in a hallway redolent of gombô, sirloin roast and Creole sauces as they passed the open door of a blue papered private room and applause burst from the couples within.

So far in the past of his daughter's young life was the captain's departure that she had remembered him only from his stern visage in the great oval photograph that hung next to her dead grandfather's in the foyer of their home. The portraits were the work of Mr. Mathew Brady, celebrated photographer of the wretched war that laid waste to so much of the South. To the imaginative girl, the faces behind the bulbous glass were effigies etched on the eyes of an enormous bug. That her father was handsome was a wonderful surprise given the bad dreams of him inspired by the grotesque insect.

The last spoonful of sorbet exploded in the girl's mouth with an effusion of most flavorsome orange. Putting the spoon down, she picked up the packet of papers.

Begun in 1907 with a shipment of cotton to Le Havre, her father's journey unexpectedly sprouted a second leg, from France to Shanghai, the hold stuffed with fine apparel for the ladies and gents of that town's upper crust. After replacing a cracked boiler flange, a third leg took the ship to Australia with a cargo of Chinese silver goods bearing counterfeit British hallmarks. In Melbourne while awaiting a substitute for the boiler itself, which was fast succumbing to rust, the captain arranged to add a fourth leg to its improvised itinerary. For it, the manifest showed but one item, a person, an elderly native of Milan and his seven male servants. At the teeming, disorderly port of Singapore, that gentleman disembarked with his retinue to return in the fastness of night with three sea chests on a wheeled flatbed drawn by coolie porters. A tail was subsequently added to the four legs when at dawn the ship left for Milan.

Behind the celebratory greetings at Lippard's was a rumour that began its race through the city moments after the ship docked. It claimed that the captain was in possession of three trunks chockablock with high quality pearls. The story had it that the pearls' owner died one perilously hot and windless night as the ship lay in the Great Bitter Lake bypass awaiting its turn to enter the northern channel of the canal at Suez, and was given a Roman sea burial there with the captain reading the committal prayer. The ship continued to Milan where the captain paid off the dead man's seven bodyguards, generously, according to the rumour, and ordered a handful of pearls fashioned into the necklaces his wife and daughter now wore. He then put the new boiler to the test by hurriedly steaming home with the booty.

The child perched with perfect posture while a girl of perhaps eight, wearing a soiled blue middy, removed her sorbet coupe and her mother's then gathered up the dinner plates that lay piled at a corner of the table. On her plate no trace of creamy sweetbreads on chard remained.

The pearls in her necklace were not the typical bluish-grey or diaphanous white but a mix of blacks and various shades and gradations of pink and yellow. Against her bleached muslin dress their effect, as her father had said, could only be described as theatrical.

Quoting the poet Coleridge, his note accompanying the gift read, prettily: "Benevolence is the silken thread that runs through the pearl-chain of her virtues."

She was hesitant to look at him directly. She thought she might evaporate like rain because it would be the same as staring at the sun. She contemplated objects near his face, the carnation in his lapel, white as snow in a storybook, and the wine glass that rose from the table and remained suspended inches from his lips while he replied to a comment from her mother.

Turning away, she glanced at the square of night in the open ventilation window in the corner below the low ceiling and wondered if she'd grown too big to squeeze through it.

With her father and mother talking, she had the book of smoking papers to divert her. On it was a list of awards won by its maker, La Croix *Fils. Exposition Universelle*, Paris, 1900, two grand prizes. Bruxelles, 1880 and 1888. Anvers, 1885. Amsterdam, 1883. Paris, 1889, *Medaille d'Or. Medailles d'Or et grandes Diplomes d'honneur,* New Orleans, 1885. She was delighted to see her city's name.

Even for a well-bred child, it was not easy to remain silent for long. "Where was the first rolling paper made, father?" she asked.

"What was that, my girl?" he said. "What are you asking me?"

"The first rolling paper, father. Everything must have a first, mustn't it? So, of all the papers like yours in the world, where do you think the first one appeared?"

"What an odd question."

"Yes, father, but where, do you think?"

"Child ..." her mother cautioned. She laid a fingertip on the back of the girl's small hand and kept it there. "Her mind is monstrously untamed, I'm afraid, Laurent. You must think me deficient in her education though I've tried to fill her head only with notions of duty and respect and knowledge of the virtues."

"I'm pleased with her imagination," he replied. "Many people value imagination more than you do, my dear Simone. From the lowly rolling paper to the magnificent steam ship, the world's inventions have been dependent for their inception on nothing more than the so-called empty heads of dreamers. Where do I believe the rolling paper was invented?"

"Yes, father."

Her mother took her finger away.

"Why, I would suppose in a city much like ours but constructed of paper. How is that for an answer? Does it suit you?"

"Indeed, father; yes, it does."

"You're indulging her, Laurent," her mother said.

"You don't know how often, at sea, I imagined doing just that, Simone." Then he added: "Though I was never able to picture how beautiful she has grown."

The spot on her cheek where he kissed her at their re-union that morning was again red as a rose, she was sure. "But father, wouldn't a paper city burn when a cigarette was lit?"

"Ha ha," her father said. "How clever you've become."

He went back to talking with her mother about things that didn't interest her. Before long she interrupted again. "About the papers, father. Really, where do you think ...?"

"Please," her mother said. She put her finger on the girl's hand again, pressing somewhat firmly this time.

But with humour deepening the wrinkles in the weathered skin at his eyes, Laurent answered his daughter. "Perhaps the papers were spontaneously generated, as some hold that life itself originally was."

"Indeed, father?"

"Shame on you, Laurent!" her mother broke in. "Life spontaneously generated. What nonsense rubbed off on you in the Orient?"

"Not in the East, my dear Simone. The hypothesis that life sprang spontaneously out of a primordial protoplasm is blazoned in our own scientific circles."

"What did life spring from, father?"

"A primordial protoplasm. A jelly, let us say, that contained the essence of all that is alive before anything was alive."

"Mysteries and occultism! I repeat, Laurent: shame on you."

The jelly was unimaginable to the girl, yet troubling. She tried distracting herself by fingering her necklace as if it was a rosary but her curiosity couldn't be contained. "Did pearls come from the poto plam, father?"

Resisting the urge to repeat the word so that her daughter could hear it again, correctly spoken, Simone said emphatically: "Pearls do not live, child. They are formed. You know that. You know how pearls come to be."

"Yes, mother."

Her father said: "Your mother is right, of course. Pearls aren't alive. They are objects produced by nature for the purpose of adding resplendence to the women they adorn."

The *women* they adorn! She might have swooned from happiness at her perceived elevation of importance in his eyes had not the restaurant's cat, orange and plump, come through the partially open door to attract her attention. As it passed her chair she reached for it but it stepped around her outstretched fingers and ambled back to the hallway.

The captain tugged the tasseled red cord that hung by the venting window. When the waiter arrived he asked for seconds of ices for the ladies and a snifter of cognac and a cup of coffee for himself. Thin and quick, the waiter bowed and left.

A man with a badly pocked face, unruly hair and the bearing of a soldier appeared in the doorway. Interrupting her parents' conversation, he asked gruffly for an appointment with the captain at the shipping company's office first thing next morning. A woman whose mass of hair sat upon her like a reddish shrub peered over the man's shoulder. Her eyes grew large as they focused on the girl's necklace.

When the pair withdrew, Simone complained: "For two years, Laurent, that man Ratelle has called at our house once every month to demand what he says is his due."

"And only Ratelle? I am surprised."

"I fear him, Laurent."

"He is no one, my dear. A man easily managed."

"Men change with time," she cautioned. "They grow more courageous the longer they feel they are owed something. And you intimate that there are others who feel as he does?"

"None of consequence," Laurent assured her. "The consortium did all it reasonably could to aid the failed members. They may suppose they're still entitled to share the profits but no magistrate in the parish would order a penny devolved to them."

The waiter placed the sorbet and the cognac before the guests, retreated, returned with the captain's coffee, then bowed and retreated again.

The child watched the roly-poly goblet of tawny, awful smelling liquor rise almost to her father's lips before lowering her eyes to the sorbet, which was much too beautiful to eat yet too tasty not to.

"Ratelle's visits disturbed me," her mother continued. "He is a cantankerous person constantly on the point of rudeness."

"I'll have Martin with me in the morning. If that scoundrel won't accept the truth from me, which is that he's simply a victim of the normal vagaries and perils of commerce, he surely will when he hears it from the mouth of Louisiana's foremost lawyer. He will leave us alone after that."

Not entirely reassured, Simone turned her attention to her quickly melting sorbet.

"Were you ever at Anvers, Papa?"

"Why, yes, little one. As fate would have it, I was. For a day. No more, no less."

"You arrived at noon and left at noon?"

"I arrived at two and left at one."

"So, you were an hour short of a day."

He was pleased to be distracted from Ratelle and a problem that had been resting in the back of his mind as a someday concern but was now in the foreground looming large. He'd seen the avarice in Ratelle's eyes, and his woman's, as they feasted on the necklaces. "What would you like to know about the town of Anvers, my ever inquisitive child?"

"Were you at the exposition?"

"The exposition?"

"Yes, father. You see? Here on the packet. *Anvers, 1885*. The makers of your cigarette papers won a prize. Were you there in 1885?"

"Aha, therein lays the secret behind your precocious interrogations! Expositions are shows where new commercial productions are introduced to the world. The best products of their kind receive awards."

"The birdcage that won the award … Could we buy it to replace the one where poor Feathers and Beak live? It's so small."

"Commercial productions," Simone sighed as Laurent gazed fondly at their daughter. "Wait 'til you discover how dangerous, noisy and filthy our city has become with the proliferation of the automobile. The curtains must be washed so often that the maids complain. They rightly lament that in the twentieth century there is a deal too much that needs doing in a day of work."

"And yet the automobile …" His voice died away.

In the silence of her father's private deliberations, the child asked if she might take off her string of pearls. Her mother undid the clasp and the girl received the precious adornment in her cupped hands as if a star had fallen there.

She hadn't known pearls were anything but white. Only after her father explained how rare coloured pearls were had she warmed to them.

Holding a lustrous pink one to her eye, she was reminded of a ball gown. In one of the yellows was a faint sunrise. In the soft iridescence of another she saw the full moon that always delighted her when it visited her window. At first nothing came to life in a shiny dark one but closing her lids to a slit and concentrating very hard, she made out a black sail on the sea at night. Perhaps a boat was carrying secrets about the British to General Jackson before the fight at Chalmette's plantation. Two other Tahiti black pearls, as her father called them, were in truth deep blue while another was darkest green. It was the first chance she'd had to examine them so closely.

She drank the last of her water, put the necklace in the glass and then interrupted her parents' discussion of the repairs their house required to ask for her mother's jeweled brooch. She was given it to keep her occupied.

The waiter darted in then backed out as if he'd mistaken the room that called him. The orange cat seemed glued to his heels.

Though the child knew the brooch well, she looked with greater interest than usual at its variously coloured jewels before placing it in the water glass with the pearls.

"Father?" she interrupted again.

"My child?"

"In your cufflinks ... are those diamonds?"

"Yes, my dear." He raised his sleeve to display one fully. "They're from India, the land of the diamond."

"May I see them? If I look closely perhaps I'll see India."

He chuckled and gave her the cufflinks despite his wife's frown.

The girl dropped them into the glass. One came to rest atop the brooch, the other fell past it to mingle with the pearls. Rubies glowed in the gaslight as she held the glass at arm's length. She was the Statue of Liberty, the pride of New York City.

When the middy-clad servant girl entered the room at the speed of a catamount and leapt at Laurent, he instinctively raised his arms to shield his face from attack. Using his thigh as a step for her bare foot, the girl clambered onto the table. Simone shrunk back as her husband's coffee cup was overturned, spilling its contents toward her. They were all confused. If the girl was sent to collect the empty sorbet coupes, what could she possibly be doing up on the table? Had she gone mad?

Simone shrieked when the glass filled with jewelry was snatched from her daughter's hand then watched in shock as it flew out the ventilation window. Though it seemed the girl in the middy could not possibly fit, she planted a foot on Laurent's shoulder and, barely avoiding his grasp, sprang to the opening and slipped through it as if she had been rubbed with lard.

The captain's wife regained her wits. Astounded and appalled, she yanked the tasseled cord to summon help while screaming: "Take out your pistol, Laurent! Hold it to the opening and shoot into the yard! Shoot, Laurent, shoot!"

The child pinched her eyes shut to defy the temptation to witness the intention she feared was to be read on her father's face.

A man with wavy hair looked in from the hallway. "Welcome home, Laurent," he said with bitter sarcasm, which went as unnoticed in the distressed room as he did. The woman with the clump of reddish hair peeked in next. Her corrupt smile also went unseen.

That night the captain's ship was set alight. Roused from sleep, he was rushed to the fire in a police buggy.

He recognized spite and envy in the flames. He imagined he could post a man's name on each piece of rigging that met the river with a taunting hiss. The fire tug stood by, its pumping mechanism idled by some malfunction.

The loss was a setback for the captain but he was resilient. He regretted not carrying more insurance on the vessel but by mortgaging his house and selling certain possessions of value, he raised the capital to purchase controlling interest in a larger ship not many years old. His first cargo was cotton for France.

Afraid that her parents might be forced to lie if she asked, the girl would never know for sure if she heard a pistol's grim retort when her mother commanded her father to shoot the thief through the ventilation window or if the sound was an illusion created by her violent heartbeats.

While the ship burned to the waterline, she suffered through the first occurrence of the nightmare that was to haunt her through the years.

Kneeling among decayed magnolia flowers in a desolate moonlit garden, she watched jewels cascade from a cornucopia. They were the gifts from all the wonderful birthdays and every sumptuous Christmas she would enjoy in the future. They sparkled and shone deliciously but she had to get rid of them. She had to make them disappear.

Her small hands brushed them away only to have more spill toward her. Sweeping faster and faster, she worked herself into a frenzy. Still they came. She was nearly mad with frustration. Then bright blood erupted from her chest. Becoming perfectly still, she watched the blood spread across the ground, mercifully engulfing the jewels and extinguishing their glitter.

Not a weed, not a petal, not a pearl remained.

She was eager to wash in the purifying blood. With a great letting go of tension she threw herself forward.

Realizing she was dead, she woke up, screaming.

Acknowledgements

Some of these stories first appeared in:

Bandwagon: *West Coast Line*

Coconuts, Hot Sauce, a Pig Snout in the Stew: *Other Voices*

Tracie's Revenge: *Great Canadian Murder and Mystery Stories*

Soft & Easy, Hello or Goodbye: *Alberta Views*

What Happened to the Girl?: *On Spec and On Spec the First Five Years*

* * *

The author would like to thank the Alberta Foundation for the Arts for its support.

The author would like to thank the following for their love, encouragement and food in a trying time: Julia Bell-Bowie, Jennifer and Patrick Chick, Shary Cooper, Connie Zerger, Gordon Pengilly, Cathy Ostlere, Fred Stenson, Pamela Banting, Cheryl Foggo, Clem Martini.

Previous Publications/Quotes

A Destroyer of Compasses (Guernica, 2003):

Wade Bell knows Spain as only a confirmed expatriate can ... assured and sensual portrait of a culture. (He) offers precise and ironic examples of human idiosyncrasy. Stories emerge as gems ... sharply rendered.

– Jim Bartley, *The Globe and Mail*

The stories steal upon you quietly. They do not seem, on first glance, to be dramatic, and their prose does not call elaborate attention to itself. But both their drama and their expressiveness are powerful.

– *University of Toronto Quarterly*

Characters who get out in the world to mingle and take chances ...

– *Front & Centre*

Bell invites the reader into the lives of Canadian and American artists living in Spain ... the true lifestyle of the ex-pat bohemian. Love comes and goes, on the wings of jet planes or sleeping in a rusted Citroen ... language that expresses the experiences of the artist's life in exile that they would choose for themselves.

– *The Ultimate Hallucination*

A nuanced world where people spend much of their time attempting to connect and yet wind up alone, victims of misunderstandings that can't possibly be fixed ... not in this lifetime and not over the span of more than 500 years.

– Michael Mirolla, *Event*

Bell's observations about the human animal are acute and keenly felt.

– Anne Burke, *Prairie Journal*

No Place Fit for a Child (Guernica, 2009)

Bell crafts vivid emotional and geographic terrains in his latest short fiction collection set in locations ranging from the Yukon to the historic Andalusian city of Granada. He showcases a set of predominantly male protagonists struggling to understand their changing place in society. In some cases drink and desperation are the modi operandi, as in the portrait of a Toronto family in the process of disintegration. Elderly coupledom is examined in close detail in [a story that] subtly conveys the mutual affection that can underlie ceaseless bickering. The most affecting stories eschew plot mechanics in favour of an amplification of the sense of place and its impact on characters' drives and identities. For instance, the opening story, "Mountains and Rivers and an Arctic

Sea," describes the thought processes of a young boy who assists his father ferrying passengers across a glacial Rocky Mountain lake. Bell creates something eerie and atmospheric here, elevating the water and mountains beyond their status as expected CanLit motifs.

– Shawn Syms, *Quill & Quire*

THE TENANTS OF THE HÔTEL BIRON

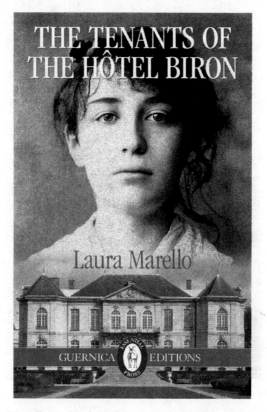

Laura Marello's novel "brings us a perceptive and unique understanding of the people whose lives crossed in the Hôtel Biron: Rodin, Claudel, Picasso, Satie, Matisse and other fascinating characters from that time. This is a compelling story on a real and imagined Paris – the ravishing bohemian Paris of the early 1900s." – Award-winning writer Jennifer Clement.

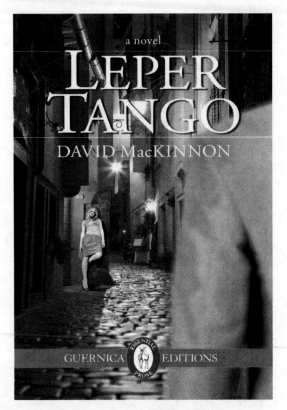

Leper Tango recounts the lunar trajectory of Franck Robinson – a self-confessed member of "the despised and despicable sub-species of skirt-chaser known as the john". During one of Franck's regular free-falls into the Parisian night, he meets Sheba, who moves from being Franck's favourite hooker to being Franck's obsession. Leper Tango is a confession of an unrepentant man whose stated life aim is to screw an entire city. The author, David MacKinnon, presumably the alter ego of Franck, is also a jack-of-all-trades and vagabond spirit.